Metaphorosis

October 2019

Beautifully made speculative fiction

Also from Metaphorosis

Score – an SFF symphony

Reading 5X5: Readers' Edition
Reading 5X5: Writers' Edition

Best Vegan Science Fiction & Fantasy

Best Vegan SFF 2018
Best Vegan SFF 2017
Best Vegan SFF 2016

Metaphorosis Magazine

Metaphorosis: Best of 2018
Metaphorosis: Best of 2017
Metaphorosis: Best of 2016

Metaphorosis 2018: The Complete Stories
Metaphorosis 2017: The Complete Stories
Metaphorosis 2016: Nearly Complete Stories

Monthly issues

by B. Morris Allen

Susurrus
Allenthology: Volume I
Tocsin: and other stories
Start with Stones: collected stories
Metaphorosis: a collection of stories

Metaphorosis

October 2019

edited by
B. Morris Allen

ISSN: 2573-136X (online)
ISBN: 978-1-64076-149-0 (e-book)
ISBN: 978-1-64076-150-6 (paperback)

Metaphorosis
a magazine of speculative fiction
from
Metaphorosis Publishing

Neskowin

October 2019

Darling

Kathryn Weaver

The damned shadows did me in. They should have been blue. Yellowish light should cast blue or violet shadows, every artist learned that. While disregard for basic colour principles was new and exciting in paint, in life it was awful.

This evening, the gallery's shadows were an unsavory shade of red, somewhere between *wine vomited down the balustrade* and *the bloodstains I tried to suck out of my only silk waistcoat.* Worse, no two of them lay at the same angle. The wrongness of it was sickening. Rather than lean on a wall, I wrapped one arm beneath my ribs and hoped the hallucination would wear off soon. They never lasted more than several hours.

When Lady Aloysia approached me, I assumed she was another figment. Of all the people from the London scene—her? Here? Now? I remembered her as a prickly, puny creature, always picking at a scab. This woman was no less small, her features sharper, if anything, but the elegance was a surprise. Her hair was pinned up in heavy auburn coils, as severe and shining as her black gown. Her chin was high, her gaze level.

She would have grown up, of course. She'd been married and gone for years. Only a hallucination, I thought, could account for her reappearance.

Then she spoke. "Why are you staring at me, Mr. Darling?"

"So it *is* you." I swept her a bow. My stomach lurched as the shadows bent with me. "I hadn't known you were in Austria, else I'd have dropped you a line."

"No, you wouldn't have," said Lady Aloysia. "But I understand you are attempting to be polite."

Ill as I felt, falling into the old style of banter was easier than not. "I wouldn't make the effort for just anyone."

"Isn't it fortunate, then, that we both decided to attend this party? Otherwise our paths might never have crossed."

The opening of a new exhibition drew out Vienna's rich avant-garde, wasps to the golden dome of the Secessionists' hive. I might have had work to show if I were in better shape. I could hardly paint when I was cursed with a reality intent on making itself art.

I ought to have tried consulting a magician sooner, but there weren't many of them, especially of a decent caliber. Now I'd come across one of the finest. If anybody could help, it was Lady Aloysia.

Of all people, I thought again, with fresh suspicion. I'd been caught in her chains of coincidence before. Best to ride it out and hope nothing too dreadful happened, though nothing ever had. Well, not to me. Not because of her.

"What brought you here?" I asked. "To Vienna, I mean. The gallery. Both?"

"Blame my husband," said Lady Aloysia. "He's convincing someone or other to part with a certain 11th century ivory casket. It supposedly transformed severed fingers into rubies. You?"

"Vee got me an invitation to show my paintings here, two years ago. On that very wall," I added, gesturing to where my demon-saints once clawed after redemption. The present offering was a lascivious bounty of flesh and gold, whose frame cast its shadow upward instead of down. I gave it a wry smile. "He expected me back in England after the exhibition."

"And Vladimir's expectations must be defied." Ah, yes. Lady Aloysia spoke from experience. With careful detachment she asked, "You are happy?"

"Ja, danke, mir geht es gut," I replied, "though I wish my German were better."

She fixed me with a long look. "You can tell me the truth later."

When I returned the question, she pointed out her husband, the Honourable Alexander Selwyn. He stood some ways apart from us, deep in negotiations with an equally blond and bearded captain of industry.

"Alexander collects antique instruments of the occult," Lady Aloysia explained. "The artefacts themselves are none of my concern, but their collectors..." She released a tense, slow breath. "He believes I am of use."

As she watched her husband laugh, I watched her. How poised she was, and entirely still—less like a statue than a hunting falcon, proud of her hard-won patience but resentful of its necessity. She wasn't happy, either. This was her way of admitting it.

"Never mind that magic is not for purchase. One might as well put a price on infinity." Her lips thinned. "And there are far better ways to dispose of such large sums."

"Rent," I suggested. Mine was three months behind.

Lady Aloysia tilted her head at me. After an awkward pause, during which I failed to find any words, she turned back to the art.

The painting before us lent its colour to the room. One figure's cheek was a tender, burning, cadmium red, as though the skin were scrubbed off. The vertebrae were picked out in gold. The ribs were stark in Chinese white and Prussian blue. It would fetch a magnificent price.

Lady Aloysia waited for me to share my artist's opinion.

"It's good," I said.

"Yours are too."

There was no responding to that.

Though I had called in my last favour for an invitation to tonight's opening, all I'd done with it was scurry away from the nice gents who might secure me a commission. *They won't remember your work*, a voice within myself had hissed. *You haven't finished a piece since, oh, when was it, 1906?* As soon as I'd arrived, I'd spiraled into another bout of self-pitying self-hatred—why try to rescuscitate such an obviously dead career?—and the shadow-curse came upon me once again.

Now was not the time to dredge up this pathetic nonsense.

"These objects you mentioned," I said, finding another subject, "how many of them are forgeries? It'd be rather simple, I should think. Find an antique, draw up a faded letter or two, a bill of sale, make it special. Anyone could do it. *I* could do it, even."

An awful light entered Lady Aloysia's eyes. "We could."

"I was joking. Wasn't I?"

"I am not," she said. "Who do you suppose is meant to gauge the authenticity? Not of the artefacts, but of the people selling them."

I followed her gaze to Mr. Selwyn and Austrian capitalist.

"That gentleman there, then," I said, imagining myself in the Austrian's shoes.

That they stood atop skewed red shadows was beside the point. "Is he playing your lord and master false?"

"Oh. Him? I cannot say that I care."

Though I did not particularly care about her husband's enterprise either, Mr. Selwyn was a stranger to me. I bore him no grudge. Yet I had no other talents, no other way of placating my landlady short of selling myself, for which I was a little old, and I hadn't got the local slang.

"Don't tell me you think it wrong," Lady Aloysia said. "You once declared you had the moral backbone of a jellyfish."

It had not been my finest moment. "There's still some squish," I admitted.

"If it will satisfy any newfound scruples, I will donate my share to charity."

At least some good would result from this business, then. If we tried it, but I knew Lady Aloysia's decision was made. Impulsive though she was, she always followed through.

And I did not like to say no to a magician so bent on conducting another of her experiments. Her hypothesis was always, *Who will stop me?*

No one, the only acceptable answer.

Having parted ways with the Austrian, apparently successful, the smiling Mr. Selwyn rejoined his wife. She introduced me as Mr. Nicholas Darling, an old friend.

That was one way to describe our acquaintance.

I ignored the memory of Vladimir's whine: *Darling Nicky, don't be jealous of my girl.*

We exchanged pleasantries, botched utterly on my part when I rambled through another wave of shadow-induced nausea, but Mr. Selwyn laughed and laid his hand on Lady Aloysia's rigid back. As he escorted her to the next room, she raised her voice to say, "You know, you might have another portrait done..."

Having made up her own mind, Lady Aloysia assumed my collaboration was a matter of course. I supposed it was. No other plans appeared on my barren schedule.

She and I next met at an antiquarian bookshop whose offerings Mr. Selwyn disdained as *too new*. I would have tried the auction houses first, but as one would expect, they were too often frequented by Mr. Selwyn and his fellow collectors.

They went to be sociable, Lady Aloysia told me, or to acquire more commonplace pieces. The gentlemen would conduct their other transactions privately—and, if they were so fortunate, with Lady Aloysia as facilitator. Her husband lent her talents to his friends.

"What do you do to the liars?" I asked as she and I poked through the shop.

"I request the truth."

I blanched. "*All* of it?"

"When necessary."

It was a heavier penalty than I'd expected. First, I recalled, she would reel out whatever scum floated at the top of her target's mind. Then she would tighten the string, let the doomed bastard keep talking, talking, until he had dredged up all the filth of his soul.

"If it comes to that, I'd rather you just kill me," I joked, in response to which I received an inscrutable blink. Lady Aloysia had always been too damned serious, too inclined to see meaning in every thoughtless little thing. I tried again. "What sort of object are we looking for?"

"Something." She led with her chin into a sharp turn. "We will chance upon it eventually."

The odds seemed unpromising. Even a small bookshop might hold infinite junk.

"So," I began, and then hesitated.

Following my gaze to the shopkeeper, Lady Aloysia understood. "Sprechen Sie Englisch?" she asked. The man bowed his assent. She tugged at her glove and nodded, satisfied. "We are speaking too quickly for him to understand us. Go on."

"I was only wondering whether you'd decided to defraud your husband before the honeymoon, or after."

That almost got a smile out of her. "I knew I would do something with him when I married him. I had not decided what. I wanted to remove myself from Vladimir, and Alexander was going to Hong Kong. It seemed almost far enough."

I wrinkled my nose at an old volume of poetry.

"We went to Paris after that," she continued, laying a finger on the book—as if shushing it—and shaking her head as she moved past me. "Then Rome, then Berlin. Now Vienna. I haven't been home for six years. He'd only returned to England long enough to acquire a suitable wife. He got me instead, but that was his own fault. As I said: I am useful to him." She pivoted, suddenly, and looked me in the eye. "How were things in London? Before you left."

"Terrible, thanks for asking," I answered. It was only reflex. Not magic.

Quickly, I moved on to the other people we had in common. Ruta Wolf had got herself jailed at another suffrage demonstration, Tristan Bell was illustrating fat pink cherubs to advertise ladies' skin creams, things of that nature. Lady Aloysia seemed willing to listen, even though my news was years out of date. I'd stopped corresponding with my friends when I'd stopped having any success to share.

As I talked, I felt as though I were toeing the edge of some enormous crevasse, a split down to the bones of the world.

"You needn't tell me about Vladimir if you don't want to," she said.

She was not so very changed from the Lady Aloysia I remembered. That girl had never failed to make a conversation as uncomfortable as possible.

I shoved the poetry book onto the shelf. "I don't."

"I am reminded of several points in my husband's favour. He is not cruel to me. He does not live beyond his means. While he enjoys certain risks, he keeps his various speculations well in hand. He has got far more money than is necessary for any one person, which you and I will shortly help to address." As if in salute, she set her black velvet picture hat at a more rakish angle. "At any rate, both he and I are ambitious, even though our philosophies are opposed."

Lady Aloysia's escape had turned out better than mine. She'd married into a career, of sorts, and gained a certain renown. Redistributing her husband's wealth—for charitable purposes, so she said—would be a nicely drastic rebellion, though if all went well, he'd never know she'd defied his control.

As her fingers danced over a row of leather spines, shadows roiled beneath them with almost puppyish enthusiasm. *Yes*, I thought at them, *I do notice the subtle play of light on the gold tooling, since you simply must draw attention to it.*

I wondered, then, how to explain the curse so as not to elicit her pity. Could I phrase it as a curiosity, a challenge? She'd appreciate an analytical approach.

I was still working up the nerve to ask her when she knelt before a low shelf and murmured, "Aha."

I could wait.

Every bookshop of this kind seemed to have at least one corner devoted to miscellaneous bric-à-brac. From the pile she selected a lone chess piece, a carved amber ram's head with a rose inscribed on its base. Eighteenth century, I guessed. I could not tell whether it was a bishop, knight, or rook.

"Not much of an enticement without the set," I pointed out.

"Unless it was cursed and cast away," Lady Aloysia replied.

It cost only ten kronen. I stared as she gave the shopkeeper the remainder of her month's allowance, equivalent to about one hundred pounds. His thanks were profuse and astonished.

"Alexander is generous with his spoils," she said to me, "but I am not in need."

"You could save it," I said.

She blinked again. "For what?"

"Anything you like?"

"Oh," she said. "No. Not I." As we stepped outside, bracing ourselves for the wind, she pressed the chess piece into my hand. "Remember that for yourself."

Fair, forty, and robust, a regular brick, Mr. Selwyn was not my preferred style of sitter, but that was the nature of the work. Portraiture was supposed to pay for the exhibition pieces, my gruesome, beautiful boys. For about eighteen months I'd lived carefully off the proceeds from the first show. Within the past six months, the money had almost entirely run out, and still I had failed to create anything new.

My keenest patron had always been Vladimir. I had painted him how he most wanted to be seen—in the nude, mainly, but I was committed to depicting more than prettiness. Vain as Vladimir was, he simply adored when I made him a horror. His joints fascinated me, raw knuckles and wrists, all that articulate gristle on which the eye could chew.

He was a magician. That unearthly glamour of his would sink his chosen boys and girls, smiling, to the most abject of bended knees. He felt he was owed it. Though his family languished in exile, he was also an actual prince. Artists were his court, intoxication his state.

I'd realised he was vile, of course. Vile was what I deserved. Dearest Vee agreed.

I'm lucky I found you, he'd say, brushing his finger across my lower lip. *You're wicked enough to properly appreciate me.* Because he said it, it was true.

When at last I was able to breathe without him—in the cool grandeur of Vienna where I understood one word in ten, where I could have myself to myself—I sold my return tickets to London and claimed the first empty lodgings I found. Over the next few weeks, the gallery administrators passed along eight excruciating letters to which I did not reply. Vladimir's ninth letter demanded I return the last picture I'd painted of him. I sent nothing.

From then on, I was cursed. He'd cursed me. Unnecessarily, as it happened. I was already convinced of my incompetence.

At any rate, I'd had training enough to grind out a few gesture drawings of Mr. Selwyn, having been invited to do so at his and Lady Aloysia's stylish residence. Mr. Selwyn himself met me in the main foyer, shook my hand, and then led me up the echoing marble stairs and into their flat.

Since I was there on business, I wasn't given a tour. I only caught glimpses of ebony cabinets, of geometric lamps and high, pale walls: a modern, perfect simplicity. Too perfect. Too calculated. The Selwyns had not troubled to make the place their own.

Mr. Selwyn's study—heaped with crates, cases, and account books left by some secretary or other—was the only room that had any life.

He sat across from me, bright in the yellow afternoon. Certainly, yes, he could smoke his pipe. No, he needn't remain particularly still.

He looked sceptical. "You've got to get it right, haven't you? Measure the proportions? The last fellow, an Italian I think, he'd hold up his pencil at me."

I gritted my teeth behind my smile. "Every artist works differently."

Mr. Selwyn was so kind as to share his many opinions on art. And on hounds, though it had been some time since he'd enjoyed a good hunt. "Unless," he added, with the twinkle of a favourite joke, "it was for my collection." He urged me to have a look around his study.

The sixteenth-century Venetian stiletto dagger had salted wounds with the tears of its previous victims. The bell-shaped, beaded gold earrings, of indeterminate Byzantine origin, rang in the wearer's ears whenever she heard someone say *aletheia*. The lute, the cricket cage, the rhyton—all of them had enacted various delicate vengeances.

When I picked up my pencil again, I stifled a groan. After a mere ten minutes, the shadows had stretched long over Mr. Selwyn's face. His nose cast a thick fuchsia slash across his cheek. He breathed smoke into the light, now blue.

"You're a friend of Aloysia's, then," he said, as though he hadn't been waiting the entire afternoon to mention her.

Nor did I miss the slight emphasis he put on *friend*. Would I blush? Flinch? Would I protest too heavily, assure him that she and I hadn't met above three times? Though if I really were nursing a hopeless infatuation with his wife, Mr. Selwyn would be more gratified than jealous. Poor, insignificant Nick Darling was no threat, and then—I had just seen his collection. He got a thrill out of possessing what other men could never have.

I didn't hate to disappoint him. "We were part of the same informal arts society, of sorts."

He sipped at his pipe. "Peculiar girl, isn't she?"

"She's a magician."

"Yes. Fascinating tricks, but damned unfair for the rest of us, I say. We can't fish out her secrets on a whim." He snorted.

My hand stilled. Surely he did not suspect what Lady Aloysia and I were about to do.

But he went on. "She likes you, your sort." Artists? Sodomites? "A friend of hers ought to be a friend of mine, if it pleases her to introduce us—and a gentleman must please his wife whenever he can. Of course, I've no doubts as to the quality of your work."

Another metaphorical abyss opened before me, and once again I'd been invited to dive in. Either of the Selwyns might have learned the trick from the other. What a splendid pair! He'd shown that trace of vulnerability only to lure me out. He knew I was after something from him. I had the commission, obviously, but a man in my position must be angling for more. He wanted the power of giving it to me.

Here it was, my chance to gain a substantial sum of money by fooling a man whose only actual crime, as far as I could tell, was being a pompous ass.

On the other hand, he was a pompous ass.

With false nonchalance, I said, "I was hoping to speak with Lady Aloysia, actually, about an old enchanted object I have. Do you know Prince Vladimir Koldunov?"

"That wastrel cousin of hers? We exchanged some heated words, I think, but beyond that I am happy to say—no."

If only I could so easily dismiss the man who'd ruled and ruined my life.

"He and I were quite good friends," I said, swallowing. "Once. He gave me the object in question." I described the ram's head chess piece. A rook, I'd decided. "There's an emblem on the bottom, too, a rose."

Almost imperceptibly, Mr. Selwyn's posture changed. He had a sleek, acquisitive look about him that reminded me of Vladimir, an air of feigned ease.

This, I suddenly realised, was how his portrait ought to be. The long shadows, the slender triangles of light. The stark geometry of his cheek, his nose. The smoke curling from his mouth, the windows spilling their gold at his feet.

"Given its relation to magic, I don't blame you for thinking of Aloysia—but this sort of thing isn't her specialty." Mr. Selwyn leaned back. "The next time you're here, you might bring it to me."

The rook found a new home beneath my desk, where I'd accidentally dropped it. I hadn't thought to pick it up. It was gathering an appropriate layer of dust as it soaked in the turpentine fumes. Unless I needed a gulp of air, the windows of my flat remained closed. I wasn't foolish enough to pit my radiator against the whole of February.

It was snowing when I looked out at the chilly grey street and saw Lady Aloysia descend from her car. She removed one black glove, kissed her middle finger, and tapped it on the side of my building— which she then entered with defiant confidence, daring the world to acknowledge she'd done anything strange.

I opened my door with a flourish. "I'd apologise for the state of things, but I assume your delicate sensibilities won't be offended."

"I try not to be hypocritical," she agreed.

Worse than hypocrisy, she *noticed*. Seen through her eyes, the detritus of my life was made obvious to mine. Rubbish, stained clothes, crusts of dried paint. There wasn't alcohol, at any rate. No opium either, nor any of its derivatives, a miserable dependency I'd made myself sweat out when the hallucinations began. Morphine had nothing to do with them after all.

Most of the place was filled with either old or unfinished work, including the piece Lady Aloysia had ostensibly come to inspect. In the week since Mr. Selwyn's last sitting, when I showed him the rook to his much-disguised interest, I'd only blocked out his head. I had not even begun to falsify the rook's provenance.

It was amazing how little an artist could accomplish when he woke at noon and performed his ritual self-castigation until three, at which point the sun began to set. I couldn't start anything with bad light. So, after I'd grimly masticated several mouthfuls of three-day-old bread,

I would fall into my cot and beg the shadows to let me sleep.

The cot was where I sat. Lady Aloysia could have the chair if she decided to stop prowling.

She would pick out a body's ripest innard, I reflected, as she tipped a particular canvas away from the wall I'd turned it against. Subject aside, and to hell with him, the piece was the best I'd shown. I kept it, I had to, but I could no longer look.

Nothing I'd create would ever be as good. Though I might sling oils across a canvas in some pleasant way, I had lost the ability to paint. I'd been able to do that much when I was with Vladimir. He may have disparaged my looks, my actions, and my feelings, but he always praised my paintings to the stars above. Because of him, the old unhappy Nick Darling had a career. The new unhappy Nick Darling had the remains thereof.

I had this awful picture, too, and I had its mental reproduction—its flaws painted over, oh, thousands of times, its perfections lovingly traced. It was a masterpiece of the mind. It was a torture in which I could safely indulge.

Never mind that it wasn't the picture that had done this to me, unless part of the curse was my being unable to let it go.

Lady Aloysia showed nothing of what she felt, said nothing. Neither did I. Gently, she let the canvas down.

She moved to her husband's portrait, over which I had flung a dirty shirt. As though teasing an invisible string, she rolled her middle finger against her thumb. Even this slight, contemplative movement made me uneasy.

After a time, she said, "Alexander relies more upon me than his own discernment. I know you would rather take pride in worthy work, but he'll not give it more than a glance."

"Do you mean the portrait or the forgery?"

"Yes," she said. "Are the materials sufficient?"

During her husband's last sitting, without my having asked, she'd slipped me a few sample records of provenance he would not miss—along with new tubes of indigo, cobalt violet, and crimson lake.

"You know they are."

"I know." The corner of her mouth turned upward. "Have you given thought to a story?"

"No," I said. "But let me see. *There once was a ram's head for chess, that wept blood and left quite a mess....*"

Lady Aloysia sighed. "When I said that he would not pay too much attention, I did not mean that you should stop trying altogether."

"You come up with the story, then."

"You're the one who will tell it," she countered. "I am only there to reassure my husband of your honest intentions. Don't pout. You were the one who said you could pull this off, and you ought to follow through. Finish something. It's hard, I know—I truly do, don't think I am being glib—but it will be good for you."

Just because she was right didn't mean I would admit it to her.

Our silence was filled with the ever-present rattle of the cars and carriages outside. I shut my eyes, scowling, but opened them again when the floorboards creaked. She'd knelt to fetch the rook out of its pile.

"I never thought I was particularly fortunate in Alexander," she said, holding it to the light, "but few other men would have tolerated the magic. I could make do with him. I had plans. So had he, for his remarkable wife. Very well. When expectations are small, it's easy to comply. Isn't it? But as soon as one gives in, they always grow." She set the rook on the window sill.

I had been Vladimir's willing lover. Lady Aloysia hadn't had the choice. She'd grown up as his pet, his princess, the precocious changeling child kept close upon his knee. Our parties had been no place for the eighteen-year-old daughter of an earl, even if she'd sneaked out to us of her own accord. Even if her skill far surpassed Vladimir's.

Which she had demonstrated when Vladimir tried to persuade her—and he could be very persuasive—not to marry her boring antiques collector. She retaliated, of course. In front of our whole circle she made him recite a florid and frankly obscene monologue, how he truly felt about her, his favourite girl. After a lifetime of his attentions, she was unsurprised. We were embarrassed. Vee was furious, pathetic, pained.

I stayed with him for another four years.

"I always fancied I was looking out for you back then," I murmured. "In my way."

"Now we can look out for each other."

A kaleidoscopic shadow-play bloomed across the wall. Blankly, I stared at it. Pretty though the red flashes were, like stained glass, my spirits were low enough without the curse's help. "I already agreed to this scheme. I need the money."

"You need more."

"What else is there, then? What did you read up here?" I tapped the side of my head. "Damned unnerving, you know, though I suppose that's the point."

"I did not read anything," Lady Aloysia said. "Not in the way you mean. You are clearly struggling with your art, and I want to help. I was waiting for you to ask."

I glanced at her. "You'll not think I'm just another fellow who's using you?"

"Not *just*," she said, wry. "Shall we balance the ledgers again, for our pride? If you complete something for me, either the portrait or the forgery, then I will consult with you about this magical problem you are having."

My first, perverse instinct was to refuse. How dare she outright offer the advice I was going to request on my own? Eventually. Sometime before never. But this, too, Lady Aloysia would understand,

and not only because she'd opened an eye inside my head.

Whenever Vladimir's parties had become too debauched, I'd always bribed another of the young women to hire a cab and take the drugged or drunken Lady Aloysia home. It was the very least I could have done. Jealous, Vee called me. Of a barely-conscious girl, hardly more than a child? She had never acknowledged the assistance. It must have been too exhausting to feel grateful for the help she'd convinced herself she didn't deserve.

Perhaps that was only me.

With a groan, I extended my hand. "Deal."

Her grip was firm, her little bones like steel beneath her suede glove.

"In the meantime, monetary assistance is yours for the asking. I can always have Alexander advance a portion of your commission. Or," she added, turning towards the door, "you could sell that picture of Vladimir."

Thanks to Lady Aloysia's deranged benevolence, our bookseller friend was glad to supply me with an unsalvageable eighteenth-century book on garden snails, on whose blank end-pages I had written a vague and horrifically misspelled letter. It had taken me a single hour of active effort. Though my sense of accomplishment was similarly brief, I'd expected no more from a task I'd chosen for its ease.

"I used a real quill," I said, pointing at a blot. "And I bleached the ink a bit, with lemon juice and light."

" *'Most Unfortunate Sir, I rellinquish to you this acursed Thing,'* " Aloysia read. "You have been enjoying yourself."

Had I? We were at the other exhibition space in the city, the Künstlerhaus, a bastion of the wholesome and conventional, a cage for tepid state-sanctioned culture and so on, and on, and on. Lady Aloysia had dragged me there so that I might feel the freedom of purely ideological complaint. Academic art was a waste of technical mastery, I'd grumbled, exaggerating my opinions for her amusement. Was she amused? It didn't matter.

We stood beside the balustrade that overlooked the floor below, next to the central marble staircase. No other visitors glanced at us as they descended the stair into a vast abyss.

"None of them can tell we're in silhouette, with that strong light from behind us," I said, gesturing at the otherworldly gold that issued from the galleries. "Can you?"

"No. Is that always what your visions are like?"

"No," I sighed, "no, no," as Lady Aloysia withdrew a journal and pen from her handbag.

Now was the time. I looked down. There was the abyss, dim red stars peering up from its depths. More fool was I, for daring to think in visual metaphors. I hadn't meant the curse to take them as a suggestion.

Lady Aloysia wouldn't disbelieve what I was about to say. She wouldn't explain it into nothing. Her opinion of me wouldn't turn for the worse. Nowhere would I find a more understanding ear. I'd never expected her, of all people, to be kind.

I drew a thick breath. "Since you asked…"

She documented my descriptions: the headaches, the nausea, the unpredictability. How the visions swung between affection and spite, as though a fairy from the fourth dimension were throwing a tantrum because I wasn't thankful enough for its blessings.

Her expression sharpened. "And to stop them, what have you tried?"

"I swore off morphine? And I went to an eye doctor, who referred me to a head doctor—a psychoanalyst. I presented myself as a fascinating case study, only he seemed more interested in my boring old homosexuality, so that was no good."

Talking to Lady Aloysia was far easier than to the psychoanalyst. One way or another, she'd got her hooks in my tongue. It probably wasn't magic; selecting my next words felt like grinding a mouthful of loose teeth.

"If there wasn't a logical explanation, it meant—I felt—no matter what I did, I couldn't—" I slumped over the balustrade.

"I understand." Lady Aloysia closed her journal. "I can do nothing for you."

"Well, damn."

"But." She raised a finger. "Anybody can be a magician."

The noise I made was unpleasant. "Oh, no—"

"Listen. Anybody can do magic, and magic can be anything. I was not born with talent. I made a choice, a conscious decision, and I practised." Compulsively, as I understood it. To call it choice was debatable, I thought, just as she added, "One's unconscious will may assert itself, especially if one is already apt to reinvent reality—which you do, Nick. Are you certain the magic doesn't originate with you?"

Coughing, I hauled myself upright. "I beg your pardon? No. No, he was the one who started it, he had to have done."

"Perhaps, but could Vladimir keep a curse alive for two years?"

"He's petty enough." Though he was not blessed with perseverance. "You're saying it's my fault."

"*Fault* is not the right word," she said. "Certain things in this world, or beyond it, are out of our control. We are left to carry on as best we can."

"It seems like you've got control."

"I win small battles, having accepted that chaos will triumph in the end." Lady Aloysia's mouth twisted. "Not that winning or losing mean anything to an incomprehensible, unquantifiable, and unprovable cosmic force that cannot care, feel, or think—much less about mere humans. I find the notion comforting."

Magic did not care what I mistakes I'd made with Vladimir. I did.

"I'm not a magician," I said.

"No?" She studied me. "Art is magic."

Several days later, I confronted the canvas.

I had the pencil sketches, the turpentine, the only two brushes—out of the twenty I owned—that I ever used. I had my palette, the skinned-over paints now peeled to reveal their freshly oozing hearts. Propped against the books I'd scavenged, I had the mirror.

My weak chin and hatchet nose were nothing like Mr. Selwyn's, but the basic shape was enough. An old trick. Mr. Selwyn would hate to know I'd painted his face by way of mine.

I wasn't one for self-portraits. I was meant to be the observer, not the observed. I used my body, made of myself the bones on which beauty was built. I was only the artist. At my best, I was a conduit through which the world relayed its suggestions: *Have you tried looking at me like this?* Every picture was a new reality. The truths were infinite.

Though I could accept that art was magic, the act of painting felt much the same as it ever had. I did not soar on any wings of inspiration. Nor did I fall into the depths of some trancelike absorption in which every stroke carried me to the next. Nor did I despair. I worked.

I glanced at the mirror, glanced again, and sighed. "Must you?"

My reflection was reversed. Or, rather, it wasn't. I appeared not as I'd see myself in the mirror, but as everyone else saw me. And I was—what? A slight and not especially attractive man in his thirties, heavy about the eyes, in desperate need of a haircut. I looked like myself. Just myself. Magic had gone easy on me this time. Even though the inverse angles weren't entirely helpful as reference, the lights and shadows belonged to a clear day.

"Is that all?" I asked.

The challenge went unmet.

Frustrated though I was, I could go on like this. I simply had to think harder about facial anatomy instead of just laying out the lines I saw. The mental exercise would be good for me. And I hadn't crawled back into bed at the first difficulty, even though I was forced to contemplate the fundamental structure of my unlovely self.

This portrait would be the first thing I finished—and I would finish it—in the two years I'd needed to lose. I'd had to sweat out Vladimir until I reclaimed the beginnings of the artist I actually was. The portrait wouldn't be particularly good, that I knew, but in it there would be none of him.

It was the only piece, they'd say, completed by this semi-obscure British painter during his bleak Vienna period. I could do nothing more. Not here.

Rectangles was my first impression of the Selwyns' formal drawing room, followed by my second: *more rectangles*. It would have seemed too empty but for the details, like the sparkling strips of mosaic that bordered the windows.

I was directed to a plain, graceful wooden chair. Mr. Selwyn eased onto the complementary settee, claiming the room's sole patch of sun. Lady Aloysia rang for tea before placing herself at her husband's arm.

"What an interesting use of colour." Mr. Selwyn indicated the portrait, vibrant and large. It had barely fit into the car he'd sent for me. "I had not realised—and it is no bad thing, mind—that you would be taking such an experimental approach."

Too late to change it now.

"I am so glad you appreciate Mr. Darling's eye," said Lady Aloysia.

The tea arrived. A maid poured three cups, the first of which Lady Aloysia passed to her husband. I pilfered a cake from its shapely stand.

"Now," said Mr. Selwyn, "let's see that chess piece again, shall we?"

I dug it out of my pocket and placed it on the low table between us.

"My dear, if you would?"

I recognised the stiletto, served discreetly with the tea, as part of Mr. Selwyn's collection. Lady Aloysia unbuttoned her soft white sleeve, turned over her wrist, and nicked a vein. I winced. She did not. Angling her hand, she let three drops of blood spill into her tea. After touching her middle finger to her wrist, she swept more blood around the cup's gleaming, golden rim. She laid the dagger on a saucer and tied a wedge of gauze to her wound.

Here's a hint from one professional to another, I had drawled, half-drunk, when Lady Aloysia and I first met. *You draw the knife down your wrist, not across*—in response to which she rightfully snapped, *I know what I am about.*

Shadows buoyed her hands as she lifted the cup to her lips.

Mr. Selwyn, at least, was enjoying the performance.

"At this point," Lady Aloysia continued, "I would either ask our connoisseur to test me with a lie, or I might draw some insignificant secret directly from his tongue. Then I would repeat the exercise with my husband. Since you are familiar with my abilities, Mr. Darling..."

"There is no need," Mr. Selwyn finished. "Simply tell us what you know about this piece."

Also from my waistcoat pocket, I pulled out the forged letter, appropriately brittle and foxed, and folded as though it had once borne a seal. "As I said before, Prince Vladimir—a magician himself—gave it to me. The original enchanter meant to get the better of a cheating colleague. Whoever captured this rook would fail to win any other game, ever again."

Mr. Selwyn held out his hand to receive the letter.

I cleared my throat. "Once the cheater caught on, he went to some effort, described there," gesturing, "to rid himself of it."

"Yes, I see." He skimmed what I'd written. "Very good. Though none of this is authenticated, you understand," he said, not unkindly. Panicky heat rose in my chest even as he continued, "It is often the case with these things. Nothing is certain—unless these remarkable properties should manifest, which my wife assures me is most improbable."

I tried a smile. "I'm afraid this is all I've got for you."

"And I expected no more," Mr. Selwyn said. "You haven't my resources."

He adopted the same lord-of-the-manor lounge as in his portrait. Well-rendered on my part, then. The very sunlight seemed starker around him, as though he were cut from the painting's elsewhere and pasted into this uncomfortable tableau. If this was magic, it had successfully caught my attention without any nauseating effects, thank goodness. I felt ill for entirely different reasons.

Lady Aloysia was the huntress again: her glance pierced her husband's skull. Watching her fingers twitch, I wanted nothing more than to scurry beneath one of the glossy black-and-gold cabinets. She sensed untruth, perhaps, a lie not our own. Did Mr. Selwyn suspect something amiss?

"Well." I swallowed. "Ah. If you need time to conduct more research, we could always continue this later?"

As Mr. Selwyn leaned into a show of thought, Lady Aloysia's stare snapped to me.

Sweat moistened my only clean shirt. I wouldn't blame Aloysia, I told myself. I could endure whatever penalty her husband asked her to inflict. She would oblige him. Better to be a tamed falcon than a trapped canary. I shouldn't expect her to compromise what security she'd found, not on *my* behalf.

Perhaps she'd let me off as easily as she could, for both our sakes. Mr. Selwyn didn't need to learn what she and I had lived through. She could play it so as to wrench embarrassing childhood stories out of me instead of blackmail fodder, or worse. After all, I wasn't Vladimir. I once chose to stay with him, true, but I also chose to leave.

Steeling herself, Lady Aloysia hooked two fingers beneath her bandage. There was no scab for her to pick.

Finally, Mr. Selwyn said, "No, no, that will not be necessary. I will, of course, inform you if I later find anything of interest." Seeming suddenly to notice Lady Aloysia's tension, he rested his hand on hers. "Anything wrong, my dear? Does Mr. Darling speak the truth?"

"It's nothing." She raised her chin at me. "He does."

I exhaled.

After settling upon a price of two thousand, he and I each signed two typewritten contracts. The *final sale* verbiage reassured me, especially since it meant something to him that Lady Aloysia added her own initials in blood. Further reassurance came with the two cheques Mr. Selwyn made out: one thousand for the portrait, which was rather more than he had previously offered, and two thousand for the rook.

When I thanked him, he replied, "Oh, you are quite welcome."

Everything was amiable as we shook hands. Even Lady Aloysia gamely accepted her husband's approval, a bristling blond kiss pressed upon her cheek.

Whatever Mr. Selwyn had been dishonest about was a question for Lady Aloysia, not me. Two thousand pounds were mine. Whether I had earned this fortune, or even deserved it, was irrelevant. I had freedom. The better question was what I'd do with it.

In case the subject himself wasn't suggestive enough, I called the painting of Vladimir 'Dionysos'. I could have cosied up to whoever bought it, but the thought of playing that game again was noxious to me, like drinking turpentine.

Mr. Selwyn was a far less demanding benefactor. He even lent me his car again, so that I could lug my old canvases to the auction house he'd recommended.

When the first of my pieces went on the block, I stepped into the hall for a smoke. Little luxuries were once again within my power to obtain, thankfully for my nerves. I dared not watch the proceedings, in case I should lose my mind and demand the blasted things back. No sense in seeking out reasons to pity myself if it'd only provoke more visions, which had eased considerably ever since I'd acknowledged I was their source.

I leaned on a column and lit my pipe. Shortly thereafter, the Selwyns came into view.

They were in conversation with three other gentlemen, presumably fellow collectors. It was with conscious deference that they ignored Lady Aloysia, which favour she was all too willing to return. When she noticed me, she brightened. A word to her husband, and he glanced over, smiled, touched the brim of his hat. Unwinding herself from his elbow, Lady Aloysia made her way to me.

I offered her a drag. "Here's to victory, right?"

"Hashish?" She eyed the pipe. "If Alexander weren't here…"

On cue, his wife's presence having sufficiently carried his point, Mr. Selwyn ushered the gentlemen and their business elsewhere. As they passed us, nods all around, I almost missed his murmur: "—sold me the lost rook—"

Lady Aloysia's earrings flashed as her head turned.

The men rounded a corner. She pinched the air, paused, and beckoned me to follow her.

"—for only two thousand. It'll be worth fifty to whoever has the rest of the Rosenkreuz set. The boy would've settled for less, I've no doubt, he hadn't any idea what it was, but I thought I'd do him a good turn. My wife's friend, you know—"

Lady Aloysia and I watched the gentlemen progress down the hall.

She shared my thought, I knew. We were meant to overhear him.

"Of all the nerve," I said, hissing smoke as though I were a fitful baby dragon.

As opposed to Lady Aloysia, whose hand covered a sudden wide and lovely smile. "Mr. Darling, I have a request. Bring my half of our profit—in ten and twenty kronen notes, please—to the Aspern Bridge at six o'clock, the morning after next."

"Why?"

"You will see." Absurdly, she laughed. "What a coincidence!"

The city was indigo at that hour, touched with mauve blue. Colour welled in the canal, washed over the stone lions and angels that guarded the bridge. Lady Aloysia waited along one of the pedestrian paths along either side, shielded from the early traffic. She had peeled back the velvet cuff from her wrist and, as she gazed out over the water, was idly probing the cut.

I heaved the valise I'd brought onto the ledge between us. "Here you are, madame. What now?"

Whatever she was planning had best be worth it. Not only was there the inconvenience of visiting the bank, there was the embarrassment of making that poor clerk change a thousand-pound cheque into small Austrian bills.

The wind snatched a curl from Lady Aloysia's pompadour as she turned away from the canal to face me. "First, we must ensure everything is loose."

My suspicions only increased as I helped her to separate the bundles. When it became too difficult otherwise, we removed our gloves. A stray edge bit into her finger. She smiled to herself and licked away the blood.

I sighed. "It's magic, then."

"What else?"

Shivering, we made quick work of the rest. Crisp sheaves of kronen soon overflowed the valise. Without hesitation, Lady Aloysia gathered a fistful and—as I sharply inhaled—extended her arm over the ledge. The wind picked up. She let go.

The bills winged beyond our sight.

"That charity you mentioned—would it happen to be your First and Only Church of Metaphysical Chaos?"

"Call it a tithe to entropy. I pay my respects whenever I can." Lady Aloysia tucked the loose curl into place. "It will find the people who need it."

"Or not."

Paper bills could just as well get caught in a vehicle's undercarriage, or disintegrate in the canal. Then again, there was a true thrill in disposing of so much wealth, so utterly and irrevocably. Mr. Selwyn wouldn't miss it. The struggling housewife, now, or the cab driver, or the petty charlatan—whoever chanced upon that extra ten kronen note would put it to better use.

"Precisely," Lady Aloysia said. "You understand. So." Reaching for another round, she asked, "Do you want to throw money off of a bridge with me?"

I did.

The valise was soon empty, the kronen blown away. We stood in silence, listening to a distant bell. The faint beginnings of dawn shivered in a barge's wake.

"Tell me, Nick," she said, "what will you do?"

What a relief, to have a ready answer. "Travel, I think."

"I am glad."

I shrugged. "You could leave, too. Wherever you wanted, without anyone to stop you."

"Yes." Lady Aloysia pulled on her gloves. "But we are going back to London soon. I am looking forward to it. There are so many things I can do."

Which, coming from her, was one of the most terrifying things I'd ever heard. I wished her well. Me, I was dreaming of somewhere I hadn't ruined, somewhere new. Italy, perhaps, or Greece. Somewhere full of colour and light.

See Kathryn Weaver's story "Darling" online at Metaphorosis.
If you liked it, leave a comment. Authors love that!

Remember to subscribe to our e-mail updates so you'll know when new stories are posted.

About the story

"Darling" is part of a sprawling, shared-world/co-writing project that my wife Emily and I have been developing for a number of years. The Child in the House, as we call it - after Walter Pater's Imaginary Portraits - is a series of stories about two generations of magicians and mediums. "Slip Stitch" - from the October 2019 issue of Timeworn Lit]- also belongs to this world.

This particular story derives from a wealth of personal experience: like Nick Darling, I'm a gay, mentally ill artist. I've bumbled through plenty of awkward gallery openings, and I've excreted plenty of awful oil paintings that got "accidentally" left in the studio, never to be seen again. I hope I've included a lot of details that visual artists can relate to; for instance, even painting digitally, I use the same two brushes for everything.

For the record: I deeply, truly do not recommend using oil paints in your poorly-ventilated early 20th century apartment building, especially if it was built to keep heat inside.

Speaking of the late 19th and early 20th centuries - it was a fascinating time for art and illustration, and, as you might expect, hugely influential on my own work. The Aesthetic and Decadent movements, the Symbolists, Art Nouveau, Arts and Crafts, Cubism - and, of course, the Vienna Secessionists. I'd encourage curious folks to look up not only Gustav Klimt and Egon Schiele, but also Charles Rennie Mackintosh, Otto Wagner, Hilma af Klint, and Oskar Kokoschka. Art movements are more than just paintings and sculpture. They're furniture and interior design, they're architecture, they're math, they're philosophy. The deliberate synthesis is part of what attracts me to this period in particular; the other part is sheer visual appeal.

I've listed a lot of names here, I know, but I am an authorial and artistic magpie. I am a human Pinterest board. I collect and I synthesize for the aesthetic. Even the Prince nod (Nick Darling, Darling Nikki) is intentional - I live in Minnesota, after all, but there's a reason the Purple One is one of my wife's and my creative touchstones.

I genuinely believe that art is actual, for real magic. Writing, music, painting, all of it. Art is magic!

A question for the author

Q: Do you make art other than prose? What kind, and how is it different?

A: I do! I'm also a freelance illustrator - I mostly work on pieces for various speculative fiction venues, but in addition to private commissions, I've also done print magazine covers, interior illustrations, and spot editorials. I've even contributed environmental art for a forthcoming mobile game.

I studied intaglio printmaking, oil painting, and drawing, not to mention my forays into paper sculpture, but currently I work mostly on digital paintings. In fact, I'm a more confident visual artist than writer - writing is far more personal to me. There's a sturdier boundary between myself and illustration work. While I love creating art, of course, I'm less emotionally attached to any specific piece. I'm more easily able to brainstorm - I can let things be sketchy, incomprehensible thumbnails before I polish them. When I started bringing that approach to my fiction, it improved immensely.

About the author

Kathryn (Kat) Weaver is a writer and illustrator whose written work has previously appeared or is forthcoming in Apex Magazine, Lackington's, and Timeworn Lit. She lives in Minneapolis with her wife and their two birds.

kathrynmweaver.com, @anoteinpink

Misalignment

Erik Goldsmith

When Levy Green awoke, he looked around for a few blinking moments, and did not try to remember. He was alone. Through an open window, he could see it was day. Something, somewhere was beeping. An ache began to throb in his forehead and, after a bit of searching, he discovered an unfamiliar incision just below his hairline. The words *What if I* came into his mind. *What if I what?* he asked himself and then remembered the surgery. He remembered what it was supposed to give him; what it was supposed to take away. *Had it worked?* A joy filled him, and like a child who couldn't wait on Christmas Eve, Levy Green tried to imagine killing his wife.

He discovered he could.

The knife would go in, her muscles would slack. He would catch her then, and as he eased her to the ground, he would smooth the hair on her forehead to the side like he used to. His son would be standing there watching, learning, internalizing everything.

"Mr. Green?"

Levy opened his eyes and saw a man in a white coat standing beside his gurney, glancing through a folder. Levy hadn't heard him come in.

The doctor looked up from the folder and smiled at Levy. "Hello, I'm Doctor Ajith. I performed your operation."

Levy nodded, choking back disappointment and sarcasm. "How'd it go?"

The doctor patted Levy's arm. "It went as well as it could have, Mr. Green. How do you feel?"

"I don't know."

The doctor nodded. "Lie back."

Levy let his weight sink into the gurney and felt the pressure of the doctor's fingers on his forehead.

"It looks good," said Dr. Ajith, more to his work than Levy. "The stitches are clean, no swelling. It may hurt a little, and you can expect some light bleeding, but it's nothing serious."

He called to a nurse and gave her Levy's folder. "He needs 6 months' supply of 1.25 mgs of Traxipin, 20 mgs of Vituperol, and a month's supply of Gluodioxyamphetymine."

"Okay, it looks like you're all set. Do you have any questions?"

"Six months?"

The doctor leaned forward for the slightest moment, then snapped his head back. "Oh, the medication...Yes, well... Very, very standard, Mr. Green. You'll be taking the Traxipin and Vituperol once a day for 6 months to align your subconscious with the implant, right before bed. If you know you'll be asleep in 5 minutes, take them."

"But for...6 months?" He almost said "another".

"That's right. That's right, for 6 months. Now, the gluodioxyamphetymine is a little different...try saying that three times fast, right?"

The doctor paused for a reaction, and got none.

"Anyway, the gluodioxyamphetymine is a slow drip that will stimulate higher levels of cortisol and dopamine to respond to your new moral impulses, until your body starts creating them naturally. The nurse will show you later, but there will be an intravenous line directly into your hip here." He pointed to his own hip. "It usually takes no more than a month for the Insta-Karma implant to begin working, then the gluodiox-"

"Only one month," Levy gasped. "Only one more month...then I'll know?"

The doctor hesitated before answering, though he now clearly understood Levy's question. "Well... For most people it usually takes a couple of weeks, but of course, it's different for everyone."

"But, I'll feel it when it starts working?"

"Yes, the implant is designed to alert you if the mental firmament that creates your thoughts and behavior diverges from —."

"But, I'll know."

"That's correct," said the doctor, shifting away from complexity.

"Not just if I'm right about to do something terrible, like..." he paused, studying Dr. Ajith's face for judgement, "...murder or whatever, but for any line of thinking that may lead to some other line of thinking that may eventually…you know?"

Levy had asked this question many times during the process. He had asked the Insta-Karma hotline operator, the in-store secretary, the salesman at the store, the clerk, the technician programming his morality tree, the pre-op nurse, and now here, after the fact.

"Okay, to be clear, Mr. Green, the implant does not stop thoughts per se, but it will stimulate a kind of instinctual…" the doctor rolled his hands towards the right word, "…aversion to that line of thinking."

The answer did not satisfy. Like a sinking boat, all fears needed to be plugged. Levy kept going. His voice rising in fear. "But, even if it seems like an innocent thought or experience that later opens the door to me doing something awful, it won't—" Levy clutched the bed, the blankets, the sheets at his side, tugged them close. "It won't let me—"

"Yes. Now, I don't know the specific technical aspects of it, but I believe it has that level of precision. You are guaranteed assurance."

Levy loosened his grip on the bed slightly, and Dr. Ajith's eyes softened. "It will be the new conscience you feel, Mr. Green, not the one you were born with. Here, let me show you the scar."

He took a mirror off a shelf and held it in front of Levy. "Eight stitches. Very, very minimal." Dr. Ajith smoothed Levy's hair back to let him see. Levy felt comforted by the ease with which the doctor touched him. He contemplated the intimacy. The man had been inside his physical brain and obviously felt some ownership over his body. It felt like affection.

"Do you think I did the right thing?"

Dr. Ajith didn't answer, but continued to trace the outline of the scar with his fingers. Finally, he took his hand away and put the mirror back on the shelf. "What do you mean?"

Levy frowned and Dr. Ajith cocked his head.

"Only you can know if this procedure was right for you, Mr. Green."

"Right, but..." And then Levy stopped. There was a twinge somewhere in his mind. He was about to ask whether it had been a "mistake," giving possible gravity to that which was not, but instead he felt a twinge and closed his mouth.

Levy gritted his teeth and looked away. "Never mind."

Dr. Ajith, oblivious to his patient's speculation, put a hand on his shoulder. "Well anyway, you and I will see each other in one month. And we can go over any issues you might be having, but in all honesty, I don't expect any."

He put out his hand and Levy shook it.

"Goodbye, Mr. Green. Have a good day."

"Thank you."

Dr. Ajith walked out.

Levy lay there in silence for a few moments and then brought his hands to his face, ran his fingers across his cheek, his scar and newly shaved head, trying to summon the same confident ownership of his body that the doctor had exhibited so effortlessly. But something felt off and awkward and Levy stopped touching himself. He closed his eyes, imagining all the ways he could violate his son, waiting for the implant to stop him.

Levy is 8 years old. His Mom let Dad back in. He's been back for a month.

Their Labrador, Delilah, just had 5 puppies. Four black ones and one with both black and white. A mix, his mom says. Delilah isn't a purebred. He watches them come out. Delilah licks them as Mom rushes around with a towel. Dad leans against the doorway and catches Levy's eyes when he wants it.

They let Levy name all of them. He names them after the kids from his class. Pablo, Jamil, Nick, Brie, and David, the mix. David will be easy to remember because he's the only black and white one, but the others all look the same. His mom wonders the question out loud. Levy looks at his Dad for an answer. The man smiles, shrugs and Dad tells him that Mom is *kinda dumb* and laughs. Levy doesn't want to think his mom is dumb, but tries thinking she's dumb anyway and laughs. Mom walks out of the room.

That evening Levy sits in the doorway of his room, listening to them downstairs. They are trying to be quiet tonight. She wants his Dad to start going to church with Levy and her this weekend. *Levy likes going. You should go with us.* He learns Dad doesn't believe in God. *Stop trying to turn him into you. Only idiots go to church.* Levy wonders if he actually likes going to church. Should he think that his mom is tricking him into going? He doesn't want his Dad to think he's an idiot like Mom.

He starts kicking the door frame and knows they can hear. They come and stand over him. He needs something from both of them, but he's not sure what. *It's bedtime,* they say. *Go to bed.*

His mom is on a business trip. He's alone with his Dad on the couch. They've been talking. Levy finds out that his mom likes to control people, that's why Dad had to leave in the first place. He's old enough now to understand. The phone rings. It's his mom calling to tell him goodnight. She asks him questions about his day. His Dad is watching him. Levy gives her short "yeses and nos." She asks him what's wrong. "You're what's wrong." Levy doesn't know why he said that, but his Dad laughs in agreement. This is what it feels like to be right. His mom asks him why he said that. Levy remembers to think that she's trying to trick him. "Why are you so controlling all the time?" She starts telling him she loves him over and over. His Dad grabs the phone, listens to words meant for him, and makes the talking too much sign with his hand. Levy makes himself to laugh and then his Dad hangs up the phone. His mom will think Levy did it to her. His Dad laughs and Levy forces himself to laugh too, as if he were proud of himself for hanging up on her. It was the right thing to do. His Dad turns on the football game and Levy gets off the couch. He walks into the den where the puppies are sleeping and buries his face into them. Levy knows that if his mom was there, she would tell him to be careful. Parents are supposed to stop you from doing bad things.

Mom is back at home, but Levy's not speaking to her. He's been looking for a way back to her, but he can't find one.

That evening he sits in the doorframe again. They are louder than usual this time. He hears his own name, and then, though he doesn't know the word for it, he gains an understanding of violence, and somehow it feels right, like Levy has done it, like he'd wanted to hurt his mom. Every impossibility pours into the possible, ever gaining potential, and he witnesses all the trust he ever had in himself vanish. He hadn't even known it was there, not really, not until he saw it leave. The possible, the impossible, they had always seemed so different. And he had been so sure.

He gets up from the doorframe and lies down in bed. He starts cussing at God in his mind just to see. God is supposed to stop people from doing bad things. He waits for punishment, aching with guilt, but nothing comes. He finds his mind doesn't stop. A dam breaks and he goes farther and the words "What if I" begin every thought, and every thought ends with him doing something worse and worse. He feels paralyzed by his own disgust and fear, unable to stop thinking, and yet, somehow, it still feels right. Isn't there something that stops you from hurting what you love? It doesn't seem like it. But if nothing is there to stop him, could he do something wrong even if he doesn't want to? The muffled sounds of screams and terror below – and even his own empathy for them – feel like evidence he could.

It is Sunday morning. He gets up before they do, puts on his church clothes and walks out of the house, out to a field beyond the dead end of their street. There are no cars. He is holding David, the mix. The little puppy squirms in his palms. Holding the little dog close to his chest, he carefully shimmies down a stony hill into the dry bed of a retention pond. No one stops him. David whimpers and Levy presses his face into his velvet fur. He can feel the puppy's ribs and brittle arms and legs with his cheeks and nose. The dog becomes quiet. He has to go somewhere no one can see. He needs to be sure.

At the far end of the pond, there is a large concrete tunnel. He stares at the entrance and looks around. No one stops him. He goes in. Someone will stop him.

The tunnel runs for a quarter mile under the field and ends in a large cubic space. Levy steps into the opening, relishing the contrast from the tight quarters of the tunnel. Some light filters in from four rectangular openings above near the ceiling, where rain might spill. He has been there before. He remembers watching the water cascade down onto the concrete slab in the center like some sacred altar, pooling around the edges. He would sit in the tunnel, staring at the four waterfalls, shivering from cold, and feeling guilty when his reverence turned to boredom.

David tries to climb up his button down shirt, his dewclaws catching the fabric and Levy pulls him off and lays him flat against his arm, cradling him. He runs a finger over David's stomach and he feels an emotion pass between them and the dog is still. If anyone is going to stop him, now would be the time.

He looks up toward the manhole covering, a deep rust, and waits for it to open, blinding him. It doesn't. He listens for his parent's shouts, really his mom's shouts, from far off. But there are none.

He places David in the center of the slab and crouches beside him, watching. The little dog's legs flop about and he wiggles toward Levy, unaware of the edge. Levy catches him before he falls and puts him back in the center. The same thing happens again. The dog's legs paddle against the concrete, scraping his belly across the surface toward the cliff and right before he tumbles, Levy saves him. He picks up the puppy and nuzzles the dogs face. David nips his nose again. Someone needs to stop him.

Levy holds David in the center of the slab with his left hand, not letting him move. He raises a rock. The dog whimpers. Someone is going to stop him.

"Dr. Ajith's office."

Levy pinched the phone between his head and shoulder, and put both hands back on the wheel.

"Hi, this is Levy Green, I'm calling to schedule my follow up appointment...Yes, I can hold."

"Is that Mommy on the phone?"

Levy glanced at the 3 year old in his rearview mirror.

"No, it's not Mommy, it's a doctor."

"Oh, Terry's a doctor. Is it Terry?"

"Who's Terry?"

"He's a friend of Mommy's. He said he was a doctor. You could see him."

"Did he stay the night?"

Ben blew out his cheeks.

"Ben, did Terry stay the night?"

"I don't know. Are you sick, Daddy?"

"No, I'm not sick, but did Terry stay the...yes ma'am, I'm here, next week will be fine, but I wanted to ask about something," He stole a glance at the oncoming traffic on the other side of the highway. There was no partisan separating the two lanes. "I'm not sure the implant is working."

"Daddy, Daddy, look. A school bus!"

He saw it coming from the other direction. "Wow, that's a cool bus, Ben...

No, I'm not in pain. That's part of the problem." *What if I turn this wheel to the right and hit the school bus head on?* He glanced at his son in the mirror. "It's just that I don't feel anything at all." *The bus would flip, and all the children would be thrown forward.* His hands tightened on the steering wheel. It was getting closer. He started to hyperventilate. Dr. Ajith's secretary continued on the other end of the line, but he heard none of it.

He would hear their screams. The jagged metal edges crocheted into their little bodies, the glass strewn across the road. The bus was only a few seconds away. He shut his eyes. Now or never. Levy opened his eyes. The bus had passed, and he breathed a sigh of relief into the phone.

"Hello? Yes, I'm still here…Sure, Tuesday's fine." Levy sunk in his seat, then hastily straightened back up so he could see the highway clearly. He glanced in the mirror and saw what his son had found. "I understand, yes, 8:30's fine, bye."

He hung up the phone and spoke to his son in the mirror. "No, put that down Ben, you could bend it, that's Daddy's."

A few days before the surgery, Levy had sat down with the Insta-Karma technician and programmed exactly what he wanted his future morality to be. They'd given him a schematic of it in the shape of an intricately branched tree. He'd meditated on it often in the car, his personal morality made visible. It was his only copy.

Levy quickly reached behind him and snatched the schematic away from his son. The boy began to cry and Levy put his hands back on the wheel. "That's not yours, Ben," he said to the mirror.

"Yeah, it is. That's MY TREE PICTURE!"

The crying continued for the rest of the trip. When Sarah opened the door, Ben was still rubbing his eyes and sniffling.

"Thanks for picking him up, Lev...Oh." She bent down and touched Ben's hair. "Hi sweetie, you okay?"

Ben shook his head and hugged her leg. She looked up at Levy and frowned.

He shrugged. "I took a paper away from him in the car."

"Oh that's mean, Daddy. Did Daddy take your paper away?"

Ben nodded.

"Hmm, well, why don't you go play, I'm going to have a conversation with Daddy."

"Is Daddy in trouble?"

"No, we're going to have a conversation. Go play with your trucks."

Ben scrambled over the stoop and walked into the playroom.

"You shouldn't say I'm mean," said Levy when Ben was out of sight.

She looked stunned. "I know. I was just...I wasn't—"

"Now, he thinks I'm mean."

"He doesn't think you're mean."

He shouldn't have to remind her about his childhood. "If you say it, Sarah, he thinks it."

"I'm not trying to poison him against you, Levy. And clearly, he doesn't even remember what yo—."

"Just..." He held up a hand, interrupting her. "Please."

"Okay, sure." Her voice sounded a touch tight. "But, I'd never say anything bad about you. You know that at least, right?"

Levy nodded quickly and crossed his arms, struggling to find a way back. "You doing okay?"

She looked around their porch as if to assess her own state. "Yeah, I think so... we miss you...Ben told me that you went to the doctor. I didn't get a chance to ask you about that last week, you rushed off too quickly."

"Yeah, yeah." He knew she knew about his implant. He'd talked with her about getting it, about his mental issues, far more than necessary. "It's fine."

She reached across and grabbed his crossed arms without hesitation and squeezed. It surprised him and he found himself nodding as if her touch contained every question.

After a moment, she removed her hand, rubbed it against her leg. "Okay, I was just curious." Her eyes went to the scar on his forehead. "I'd heard about it, wanted to ask."

"Yeah, I haven't felt anything...I mean, it hasn't really done anything, yet. They say it's a process."

"Oh, okay," she said and took a few steps backward and leaned around the wall so she could see Ben. Levy watched her body arc and shuffled his feet. When she came back, she was smiling.

"He has on a cowboy hat and is humping the gator, going 'ride 'em cowboy.' Come here." She stood to the side and let him step into the foyer of his house.

She was not lying. Ben was indeed humping their large stuffed alligator. "Look, Daddy, I'm a cowboy!"

"Wooo."

The boy waved his hat in the air like a bull rider. Levy shook his head and turned back to his wife to say goodbye, but she walked past him into the kitchen before he had the chance.

"You want an s-o-d-a or something?" She shouted. There was hope in her voice.

"No thanks, but I do have to go."

"Come into the kitchen for a second, I have to make his lunches for next week."

The kitchen looked clean. Far cleaner than when he was living there 6 months ago. The knives were back out. She had taken the knives back out. He saw himself stabbing her and Ben, violating both of them, the blood would cover everything. His little body. Levy pressed himself into the wall, trying not to move.

"So Lev, you haven't, like, felt anything from it?"

"I have to go, Sarah."

She ignored him. "You seem the same to me…Was it expensive?"

Levy shrugged. "Sarah."

"I heard the government offers it free to some people."

He closed his eyes, resigning himself to his own kitchen, to the conversation. "Pedophiles."

"Yeah, a friend of mine, a doctor actually, told me they've started giving it to certain prisoners for a reduction in their sentence."

Levy opened his eyes, "A doctor?"

"Yeah, you heard about this?"

He shook his head.

"Oh, I forgot to tell you. Janet told me that her husband got one...an implant, you know. You remember Greg, he had the—" She turned and pointed to her lip.

He nodded, remembering the man's cleft lip.

"Isn't that weird!" She turned back around. "He didn't seem the type, but she told me he's trying to get sober after he wrecked their car. Said he hasn't touched a drop since."

"Really?"

"That's what she said." She grabbed a knife from the rack and began cutting salami. "I haven't seen him or anything, but she says he's happier and calmer, doesn't yell at Teddy as much. She told me he watches documentaries now."

She put the knife down and got out some bread.

Levy's eyes lingered on the knife. "Is he creepy now?"

Her head see-sawed, side to side, as she did when she processed his doubt. "She didn't say, but she did tell me that..." she picked up the knife and spread some mayonnaise, "...it seemed natural to her somehow, so I guess not, I don't know."

He grunted.

"How does it work?" she asked.

He thought of saying, *What, the fucking doctor didn't tell you?* But the words screwed up inside him, and he swallowed them. "It's supposed to help prevent thoughts and beliefs that might become behavior." His eyes returned to the knife in her hand.

He could rush her and tilt her over and take her right there, knife to her throat. Ben would walk in and see all of it.

"How does it know which thoughts become behaviors and which thoughts lead nowhere?"

Levy shrugged and closed his eyes again. He couldn't trust himself with that knife in the room.. All of his muscles were tense, as if his body might start acting on its own if he relaxed in the slightest.

"And how deep does it go?" She started chopping lettuce. "Like, if Greg watched something with drinking in it, normally he'd like it, but now he couldn't like it as much because the implant would stop him?" She put the knife down and laid the lettuce on the sandwich. "I don't know. Sounds weird, Levy." She wrapped the sandwich up and threw it on the counter. She turned around; knife behind her.

"It's supposed to be more nuanced than that."

"I know." She pushed herself off the kitchen counter, afraid her casualty was offending him. "It was a stupid example."

"No, no, it's not about the example, I'm just saying..." He paused, unsure what he was saying, "It wouldn't just stop him from thinking...It's would make him aware."

She narrowed her eyes. "Aware?"

Levy couldn't meet them. "The implant would tell him."

"It would hurt him?" Her words sounded less like a question and more like a realization. "Is this thing going to hurt you, Levy?" There was panic in her voice.

She looked at him for a moment, recognizing his silence for what it was, then grabbed the knife and began making another sandwich.

"Of course," she muttered.

From the other room, he heard Ben ask the alligator if he was a cowboy like him. The alligator didn't say one way or the other.

"Just like that Clockwork movie?" She wrapped up the second sandwich and quickly started on the third. "So, it just hurts you until you are who you want to be."

"There's supposed to be a spectrum," said Levy, unwilling to grant her the summary. "And it depends on the person." Her chopping became louder. He knew it to be anger. "It's just we don't know what we're capable of until it's too late, so—"

"Sure, Levy," she interrupted. "Can you hand me some twist ties?"

He opened the cabinet, unable to stop explaining. "We like to pretend that our morality is fixed in cement, but we just...where are they?"

"They're not there?"

He looked again. "No."

"Check on top of the fridge."

He found them and placed the twist ties beside her. "Here." He stood at her shoulder. He was closer to the knife now. He could see it in her hand. There were so many things he could do with it; *so many places he could—*

She glanced up at him.

He took a step back. "We just don't know when something might make us slip up."

"Right, exactly what I said. So because *you* don't know, you're going to hurt yourself. It seems like you've already been doing that ever since Ben was born." She wrapped up the sandwiches. "I guess I'm glad you found something to do it for you."

Levy watched her shoulders, her hair. The brisk movements that signaled her frustration. He hadn't meant to upset her. They stood together in silence until she finally thought of a way to communicate less directly.

"That same doctor friend of mine also told me some parents have started trying putting implants in their children if they worried about them being gay...to program them." She said it with disgust. He knew some of it was for him.

Levy looked at the knife and then back at her. "I don't know. I didn't ask."

She picked up the sandwiches and put them in the fridge. "So, you haven't felt anything? Maybe you can stay, then."

He began to edge out of the kitchen.

"No, no, no...Levy, look, don't go yet, okay. I know that fight we had freaked you out, but people fight sometimes." Directness was always her last resort. "It didn't mean anything, and it's been 6 months. I know you thought you were doing me a favor, but I'm done with this seeing other people shit, Levy. So is Ben. Come home."

"I can't...not yet." Levy couldn't stop himself from looking at the knife again. She saw him do it, and quickly put the knife in the drawer.

"It's still happening? Are you still worrying about hurting us?"

He didn't like hearing it said out loud, like it was real. "No, no, no. It's—"

"Oh, Levy. Are you okay?" She neared him, touched him so freely, like he was air she could move through. She touched him like he was empty space, and he ripped away from her and considered asking about "Dr. Terry" and whether or not Ben liked having a new dad, but he felt a twinge inside him and instead walked out of the kitchen.

"I'm sorry, Levy, I wasn't trying to..."

"No, no, no," he reassured her from the doorway. "It's fine, I just have to go."

He turned and shouted into the playroom, "I love you, Ben. Take care of your Mom for me, okay?"

That weekend, Levy went to a bar and met a woman who came home with him to his tiny rental apartment. They fumbled in the dark and made love, fell asleep. The next morning, she tried to tell him about herself. She sat at the edge of his bed, not bothering to cover herself and talked with a cold, chipper ease that made him feel alone. Levy barely heard a word and declined breakfast. She gave him a kiss on the cheek and left, leaving him alone with his consideration.

From his third story window, he watched her cross the street and get into a cab. As it disappeared down the street, he saw a family dressed in their Sunday best ambling along the sidewalk from the other direction. They were young, two little girls between them. The father was on the phone holding the older girl's hand while the mother preoccupied herself as best she could with the smaller one's demands for attention. Levy watched them from his window, a hand against the glass, and imagined the obscenities he could shout at them. They'd look up and *he'd pull out his sex and let them see—*

Suddenly, the smaller one lost her purchase on the sidewalk and fell into the road. A truck was coming. The parents were talking to each other. Levy banged against the window, struggling to open it. He banged again. They didn't hear him. They couldn't see. He tried again and again. The latch was rusted, tiny, immovable, the glass thick. The truck neared. The driver wasn't slowing. He beat out a rhythm harder and louder, but still they didn't hear, they didn't see and he felt of himself the familiar ache of certain tragedy, the ghost of regret, and the years of grief, nooses around the hearts of everyone involved...He closed his eyes, screamed and forced himself to look again and saw the father, phone still to his ear, pick up the crying little girl by one arm and hold her still while the mom dusted concern from her dress. The driver raised a few fingers as he rumbled by. The father waved back.

Everything was still, but Levy found himself shaking in an aftermath he'd done nothing to stop. He put his hand to his forehead, hyperventilating within his tiny space until he noticed the older girl staring up at him.

While the family had busied themselves with the little girl, the older sister had taken a step back and watched everything the man in the window had done. Somehow, Levy knew she'd seen him.

He stared down at her wondering, seeing her looking at him, and waved without really thinking about it. She waved back just like her father had done to the truck driver, and they locked eyes across the distance for a tender moment before Levy realized he wasn't wearing a shirt and quickly closed the curtain.

His mom is standing in the kitchen. His Dad is still sleeping. It's late. They were supposed to go to church. Where has he been? He pulls David out of his pocket and sets him on the floor. Mom says nothing. The shakes begin in Levy's hands and tremble up his arms and he feels the intense struggle of something that cannot be expressed, something terrible. He feels his mother's hand on the back of his neck pulling him close, asking him for certainty. He does not speak. He cannot move. His forehead touches hers. For some reason, she tells him it's okay, it's okay, and Levy's sobs break and he barks out apology after apology and each one feels like evidence to the contrary, like nothing but disagreement.

"Mr. Green, sit down, sit down. How are you? My nurse tells me that you don't think the implant is working?"

Levy sat down across from Dr. Ajith and nodded silently for a few moments, clearing some space within him. "I just think that...I haven't felt anything. Different. And I think I'm supposed to, and I just needed to be sure that..." He trailed off, quietly tracing the lines of absence of everything he didn't say.

"What do you mean, you think you *should* be feeling something?"

"I mean, there have been moments this month where...I should've felt something."

"Yes? Why is that? Did you do something illegal?"

"Well no?"

"But, you have been feeling urged to do something, is that it?"

Levy winced. "No, urge isn't the right word…or maybe it is, I don't know."

"I'm sorry, Mr. Green. I'm not sure what we're talking about here."

Levy tightened in himself, quickened, noticing the details in Dr. Ajith's face. He blinked. "I just…I've had some bad thoughts about doing horrible things, but I felt nothing."

"Okay…" said Dr. Ajith, stretching the word.

"Isn't it supposed to hurt me?"

"Mr. Green?"

"Isn't is supposed to punish me or…?"

"Mr. Green."

"No, I paid a lot of money for this fucking thing and I want…" He paused, trailing off again, unsure how to proceed.

Dr. Ajith cocked his head. "I've checked over the diagnostics of your implant… okay, let me say that there is a spectrum of potential sensations that a person might experience, so, not everyone who gets an Insta-Karma implant is going to be experiencing the same thing, you know. It would be unwise, yes, to assume or expect something in particular."

Levy nodded in disagreement, "Yes, but —"

"Now hold on, Mr. Green, what I'm saying is...okay, I checked the diagnostics from the implant, here, for the whole month."

"What?" Levy sat up. "What do you mean?"

Dr. Ajith held up a folder and placed it on the desk. "Well here, I mean, we, you can see any activity within the implant."

Levy opened the folder. Numbers, words. He kept looking, hoping that meaning would find him. Dr. Ajith continued.

"Most implants, and I believe I told you this on the day of if I remember; most implants, it takes a few weeks, and in some cases at least a month before anything really begins taking effect, but... may I see that?"

Levy handed him back the folder.

"But in some cases, the implant begins working immediately. Do you see this line of zeroes here on the right side?" Dr. Ajith held up the readout and pointed to the numbers. "These indicate synthesis... complete unification of your morality tree and your central nervous system. A zero means that there are no deviations from the expectations of neural output put in place by the implant."

Levy stared at the zeroes.

"Do you understand, Mr. Green?"

Levy shook his head. He did not understand and felt a pressure both cold and terrible. "Did I do something wrong?"

"What? No, you—"

"Can I trick the implant into thinking that I'm not..."

"No, that's not possible, Mr. Green, listen to me. The implant began working immediately. This only happens if the morality you programmed into the implant was already in agreement with..." the doctor rolled his hand toward the right word, "...with you."

Levy struggled in the chair, in empty space, open air. "I've thought of such horrible things. This doesn't—"

"Look." Dr. Ajith pointed to a -1 underneath the heading CARE. "It says here that the implant activated on day one and actually provided you with the tiniest adjustment, somewhere...sometime, let's see, yes. You would've still been in the hospital at this time. Do you remember feeling anything?"

Levy was quiet.

"It says here that the only other time it activated was last Friday afternoon, see here it is, another negative one under

DECENCY. Do you remember this? A negative one would've felt like almost nothing."

The twinge — Dr. Terry. He tried to explain it brokenly. He failed.

"Well, in any event, we know the implant is working, even if it's doing almost nothing." Dr. Ajith put on a pair of glasses from his pocket and glanced over the readout. "You know, sometimes, the cognitive dissonance between who a person thinks they are and who they actually are is so wide that we have to..." His hand made a circle in the air towards the appropriate word. "Calibrate...a time release mechanism, so that the implant is not just exploding continuously inside some poor soul completely out of touch with reality." He laughed, not unkindly. "These people, Mr. Green, they genuinely want to be good, you understand? I'm sorry, that was a silly question, but their neural pathways are so different from the ones they programmed for themselves that if not mediated, they would be in constant pain."

Levy was about to speak, but thought better of it.

"They just want it so badly." Dr. Ajith touched his cheek tenderly as if it were not his own. "These people, they…we make it so the implant only works every hour, until we can be sure they won't be just constantly suffering…You see? Intellectually they know what is good, but…negative 1000, Mr. Green. A deviation of negative 1000 literally feels like an electric pulse through your brain… through your body, it's crippling…I often wonder if I am so…What was I talking about?"

"Negative 1000."

"Oh yes," Dr. Ajith cringed and sat forward, remembering. "But you are not dealing with any sort of thing like that, are you? Only twice, Mr. Green. And only a -1 deviation, which means you probably would've corrected the aberrations yourself without the implant."

"But I've imagined…" Levy pushed through, forcing himself to say it out loud. "I've imagined stabbing my family…worse. Why can I think these things and… How am I allowed to think these things?"

"Is this why you got the implant?"

"Yes."

"Have you ever talked to anyone about this? How long has this been going on?"

Levy started hyperventilating. He thought of that puppy long ago and looked at his shoes.

"Do you know how rare it is to go an entire month with only two deviations from your own idealized self, Mr. Green?"

Levy shook his head in disagreement. "You don't understand. I've imagined raping women, doing horrifying things."

"Worrying that you might do something is vastly different than fantasizing about it, Mr. Green. These are not real things, you're thinking. None of them."

Relief began hitting him, it felt the same shape as panic.

"Do you understand, Mr. Green? If there is no chance of the thought happening, the implant does nothing."

"No chance?" Levy said, the words made it real. He imagined killing his wife. It felt hollow. He said it again. "No chance?"

Dr. Ajith shook his head. "None."

Levy put his head down on the desk, sobs racked through his body like tides seconds apart. In and out. Levy felt a hand on his back.

"There's nothing you can do about it, Mr. Green. You're good."

Levy listens to his parents yelling in the kitchen. They don't understand what happened, but she blames him. She wants Dad to leave. There is fear in her voice, but he says he wanted to leave anyway. His father walks into the living room, passes him by without looking down. He goes into the bedroom. Levy watches his father's hands pack a suitcase, watches him walk out the front door. His mom asks Levy if he's hungry. He says he doesn't know.

That evening, he is standing in the doorway of the den. The puppies are nursing. Delilah is asleep. He crouches. None of the puppies notice him, except David. The puppy removes himself from his siblings and edges towards the boy's feet. Levy runs away into the hallway afraid he might hurt him for real this time, but David follows and gets caught on the door sill, whimpering. Levy watches him from a safe distance, turns to go, but then without knowing why, goes back, lifts the little dog into his arms and cradles him long after his tenderness has disappeared into boredom.

*"See Erik Goldsmith's story "Misalignment"
online at* Metaphorosis.
*If you liked it, leave a comment. Authors love
that!
Remember to subscribe to our e-mail updates so
you'll know when new stories are posted."*

About the story

I started thinking about the idea of moral certainty, and what would be a way that I could know I was a good person. Some plaque or certificate or neural implant, something that would allow me to put all my fears to rest. So, I imagined a story where someone was constantly worrying about their own potential for harm; someone who would jump at such an opportunity to restrict themselves to something external from themselves, an implanted conscience...and then, what if it didn't seem to work.

A question for the author

Q: How do you generate story ideas, and how soon do you act on them?

A: Most of my ideas are generated by looking at my own beliefs and fears, and then translating them into some kind of story structure. I suppose writing is a way of processing things I can't fully articulate.

About the author

Erik lives in San Antonio with his wife and kids. His short fiction can be found in *Argot* magazine, *Wavelength's Anthology*, and *Dragon's Roost* publications among others.

The Season of Withering

Lisa Short

Tamasin, called Abhasvar, watched from the concealing folds of her hood as the Riever and his men strode into the great hall. For a long, fearful moment she thought the Riever wouldn't stop, would mount the dais alongside Piro and throw a too-jovial arm around his neck (and perhaps break it). But the Riever did stop at the foot of the dais, bracing his legs wide apart, teeth bared in a broad grin. He'd brought six men with him, two of them grinning as unpleasantly as their master; the other four were blank-faced, their gazes darting to the orblights on the walls. Piro had insisted on the orblights and Tamasin thought now that he might have been right to do so—that sourceless, icy glow *was* uncanny, even to her. Her own objections had centered on the wisdom of exhausting himself in maintaining them; Piro was pale, to her critical eye, but perhaps no more so than usual. She hoped.

"The prince of Anmoor himself!" cried the Riever, and flung out his arms. One of the more uneasy of his men flinched back. "Your welcome, *so* unexpected!"

"Surely not," said Piro. His voice was light, thin compared to the Riever's rich tones, but to Tamasin's pride quite steady. "Captain Shal did not assure you of our hospitality?" Tamasin and Piro had spoken nothing but Imperial Un, to each other and to anyone else who would listen, for the past four weeks. Piro had come along amazingly, well enough that he'd been able to insist upon keeping Tamasin hidden for this first meeting rather than using her to translate.

"Oh, the *captain*," said the Riever, expansively. "A hard man, your Grace! And no one was more surprised than I to hear that you not only had anticipated our coming," and Tamasin didn't think it was only the glare of the orblights that lent a metallic sheen to his dark eyes, "but were actually inviting us into the keep! But pleased, *pleased*, to hear of your immediate need for a suitable heir, though saddened by your rapidly declining health, of course."

"Of course," said Piro. "The rest of your men, they are outside?"

"Quite." The Riever's teeth gleamed. "I had my doubts that you could accommodate all of them, but those doubts have been laid to rest." *As you will be*, he might as well have said aloud. Tamasin cast a quick look across the double handful of assembled court, as many of the keep's inhabitants as they'd been able to round up who could fit into the old finery and act the part. Most of them understood enough Un to have followed some of that exchange—their collective gazes still rested calmly on Piro, though. "If you'll show us to our quarters? Naturally, we'll all stay together!"

"Naturally," said Piro, and smiled a little. And astonishingly, when the Riever met his gaze, it was the Riever's grin that faltered. He recovered himself instantly, but his eyes had narrowed, and Tamasin could see that whatever end he had planned for Piro had just acquired a new degree of cruelty.

Piro lifted his hand, and Tamasin drew back the curtain over the archway behind her. The Riever's shoulders stiffened, then relaxed as a dozen or so of what were clearly servants, just as clearly unarmored and unarmed, filed silently into the hall. As they approached him, he said offhandedly to Piro, "There are thirty or so of my men outside—your guard captain as well! I'm afraid none of his men returned with him."

Piro's mouth twitched. The Riever saw it, and satisfaction softened the hard lines of his face. Tamasin's head swam with the force of her rage. Piro was speaking, and she made herself listen: "—will take you and your men to your chambers, to refresh yourselves before the feast tonight and the accession ceremony in the morning."

The Riever casually grabbed one of the women in servant's garb by the arm and thrust her at his men. Shame, as intense as the rage had been just moments before, flooded Tamasin's eyes with acid tears. She inhaled deeply, trying to force herself into some semblance of calm.

The Riever gave two of his companions an instruction accompanied by a booming laugh, and after disappearing briefly from Tamasin's line of sight, they reappeared, dragging—*Shal!* After a night of fevered imaginings of his fate, each worse than the last, Tamasin was shocked to see him alive and relatively well. Dried blood did crust one side of his face and his nose was swollen, but he was staggering along under his own power, far more hindered than helped by the men's tugging hands. They flung him forward and he skidded on his knees almost to Piro's feet.

The orblights flared, ghastly green. A few of the Riever's men cried out, and Tamasin's gaze snapped to Piro's face. He was rigid, expressionless, and as the green bled back out of the orblights, the eerie color they had lent him vanished. Even his lips were bloodless now. Shal lurched to his feet; Piro stood as well, carefully navigating the steps down from the dais, and Shal rose to offer him a steadying arm. Tamasin moved as unobtrusively as she could to Piro's other side and he leaned heavily against her shoulder.

"Come, Your Grace," said Shal. His voice was cracked and rusty, but he knew how to fill the hall with it. "The priestesses await you in the healing chambers."

Hardly—the only *priestess* as such was propping him up on one side as Shal supported his other. There had been no true priestess in Anmoor for fifteen years, not since Piro's mother had died, and the *healing chambers* were wherever Piro and Tamasin happened to be when the need arose. But the Riever had obviously grown up on the same tales of Anmoorish magic as everyone else in the Empire, and waved them away with a sneer.

The refugees had begun trickling across Anmoor's southern border three months before, with horrific tales of marauders led by a great-nephew of the Emperor himself looting and pillaging their way up the Great North Road. South of their villages, that road led to the Imperial province of Nebra, where Tamasin and her mother had settled when the latter had remarried for the final time. North, it led to only one place still within the Empire's borders, even if only nominally—icy, ancient Anmoor.

Tamasin hadn't particularly wanted to travel the Great North Road herself eleven years before. She had still been reeling from her mother's death when her stepfather had summoned her to his study and informed her that she was to go live with her unremembered father's kin in Anmoor.

"Anmoor?" she'd said blankly, staring at him. She had thought she might have misheard him—did *people* actually live in Anmoor, anymore?

They did, apparently, and her stepfather had sent a letter to them, informing them of her projected arrival some six to eight weeks hence. "Wait—my father's kin?" Tamasin had still been utterly shocked, but her brain had been trying to work in fits and starts. "I'm Anmoorish?"

"Did your mother never mention it? Well, I suppose she wouldn't have, to you. Your father's grandfather was Anmoorish —of the ruling house there, in fact."

"But..." Tamasin had begun to protest, and then had stopped. Her stepfather hadn't been looking at her face anymore; he had been frowning down at the papers scattered across his desk. He hadn't even been pretending to forget her existence; he had been well on his way to genuinely doing so already.

And so she had come to Anmoor, where she had stuck out like a speck of pepper in a sea of salt, where she had spoken not a single word of the language, not even *yes* or *no* or *thank you* or *goodbye*—not that *goodbye* had mattered much, as she'd had no other place to go. The Anmoorish hadn't been interested in her in the slightest, had likely doubted that she was genuinely Anmoorish in even that scant eighth part. She had doubted it herself, but had seen no reason to broach the topic.

Captain Lord Shal, one of the few Anmoorish who spoke Un fluently, had stuck her in the nursery with her three-times-removed cousin, the orphaned prince of Anmoor. *Prince Piranos Abhasvar*, Shal had informed her, before literally pushing her inside a grim stone-walled chamber that looked nothing like any nursery Tamasin had ever seen and closing the door behind her. What trepidation she might have felt at being so placed with a prince of anything had faded quickly in the face of the flaxen-haired little boy five years her junior, who had greeted her with painstakingly learned phrases in Un and an anxious, eager-to-please smile. It had been so long since anyone had appeared impressed with her in any way that she had forgotten to stay distant and angry, that day—and, at least where Piro was concerned—all the days after.

Now, Tamasin, Shal, and Piro made their way down one of the keep's more ancient corridors. It was barely wide enough for the three of them, and if Shal hadn't been hunched over Piro, his head would have brushed the ceiling. Piro at least didn't seem to be worsening—what was more frightening to Tamasin at that moment was Shal's obvious weakness. He was favoring his left side—kicked, perhaps; she hoped he wasn't bleeding internally. She had gotten to know all the ways people could be damaged inside, in the years since she'd come to Anmoor; that was one of the worst, and the hardest to heal.

They finally reached the old temple and the abandoned high priestess's chambers. Tamasin had found time to supervise their retreat from the keep's family quarters, where the Riever and his men were now residing, but had not found similar time to organize any unpacking; trunks and chests were piled haphazardly against the walls. At least a fire had been lit, some time ago judging from the heavy warmth permeating the air, and a bed for Piro had been set up. Shal and Tamasin steered him toward it and lowered him onto the sagging mattress. Tamasin eyed Shal pointedly; when he didn't appear to notice, she said sharply, "And you as well, please—"

"Piro first," said Shal, staring down at Piro's sleeping features. Piro had barely been awake during the last ten minutes of their journey and had waited only for his head to touch the pillow to surrender consciousness.

"Piro first," Tamasin agreed. "But it'll be easier for both of us if you're already lying down after I'm finished with him. Besides, you look like death warmed over."

His expression grew distant; Tamasin watched him at first with curiosity, then with alarm. "You can't," she said, "you *can't* be thinking of not allowing me to— we need you! We need you *well*, not, not *shambling around* while you heal the good old fashioned way!"

One side of his mouth quirked up, though his eyes never left Piro's face.

"Your bedside manner leaves much to be desired." Then his mouth straightened out and he finally looked at her. "I was thinking of conserving your strength."

Tamasin was briefly silenced by this. She hadn't the faintest idea how much of her strength the following day would require; none of them had ever done or even witnessed anything like it. Shal had read of it, and that was all. "I suppose we had better leave you visibly injured, at least," she said at last. "But I think we do need you more well than you are now, where it counts."

Afterwards, when Shal had left, Tamasin stayed with Piro and watched him sleep—it *was* sleep, now, not the unconsciousness that exhaustion drove him into on a regular basis. But not a deep sleep—as she was thinking that, Piro's eyes opened, blank and dazed in the firelight. Tamasin frowned down at him and his gaze cleared, a small smile curving his lips. "It's definitely you," he said. "What have I done now?"

"Nothing, for God's sake. Other than pass out as usual. How are you feeling?"

"As usual," he said dryly. "That's how." He paused. "Am I allowed to sit up?"

"No."

"Go to the pot?"

Tamasin rolled her eyes. "It's under the bed. At least, it had better be under the bed—"

She bent down, but Piro said hastily, "I was just joking. I don't need it." Tamasin straightened back up and gave him an exasperated look. "I'm sure it's there," Piro said, clearly intending to placate her.

"I'll know the reason why, if it isn't." But she couldn't help smiling down at him, though it faded nearly as quickly as it had come. "I still think I should come to the feast," she said abruptly.

"Shal will be there," said Piro mildly.

"And what good will that do, if you collapse?" she snapped.

"What good would *you* do? Do you think the Riever will stand back and patiently wait for you to minister to me? He'd more likely simply claim the right to rule then and there, and you along with it." Piro's fair cheeks were flushed; Tamasin determinedly looked away, jaw clenched. "Tam, I won't collapse, or faint, or anything else." The pause after those words lasted long enough that Tamasin unwillingly returned her attention to his face. Piro's gaze had turned inward, pensive. "I'd wanted to tell you, before—something about the Riever, or his men or both, I don't know—I can *feel* them." Tamasin grimaced, and a spark of humor lightened Piro's expression. "It's not exactly unpleasant...it actually makes me feel stronger. As though I could *be* stronger, as if the strength were mine for the taking."

"Well," said Tamasin, uneasily. "Perhaps it does work that way, when... we...*tomorrow*." She forced the last word out. Piro reached out and gripped her fingers tightly in his; Tamasin squeezed back, refusing to let her own ambivalence weaken her grasp.

Piro's clear hazel eyes met hers. "I hope you'll stay, after I'm gone," he said. Shock stopped her breath and her fingers stiffened in his; he brought his other hand up to cover them. "I overheard you and Shal arguing, the night the first refugees arrived."

Tamasin stared at him whitely, thoughts scurrying through her head—what *else* might she and Shal have said, that night? "Oh?" she managed. "Really?" Even through her agitation, she was disgusted with her own lack of aplomb—but lying to Piro, even just concealing things from him, wasn't a skill she had ever wanted to develop.

"You said, that if I were dead"—and it was dreadful enough that he'd heard her say that, and even more dreadful that he spoke of his own death with such resigned acceptance—"that you might leave Anmoor."

"I'd never leave you," Tamasin said intensely. "*Never.*"

"I know," said Piro. "But...I don't think you'd leave a child, or take it away from its heritage, either. Even if I *were* gone."

Tamasin stared down at their interlaced fingers—Piro's were long, startlingly white against the battered-looking brown of hers. He had beautiful hands, a lute-player's hands, she had told him fancifully more than once when they were younger. "No," she said. "If—if there were a child, I wouldn't leave it behind, and I would stay here with it." Each word felt like the bars of a cage drawing ever tighter around her, suffocating her.

"I'd leave with you, if I could," she heard Piro say, over the hammering of her pulse in her ears. "You know I've always wanted to see the Empire." His tone was deliberately light; Tamasin couldn't quite make herself look at him, but she did prod her lips into curving upward. It wasn't even that difficult; it was an old joke between them.

"You *are* in the Empire," she said. "Ignorant savage."

"I can read better than you—"

"—in the old Anmoorish syllabary, that even you northern barbarians don't use anymore—"

"You're a fine one to talk, *Lady Abhasvar*—"

They fell into comfortable bickering, and a few minutes later Piro dozed off again, mid-sentence. Tamasin's gaze lingered on his face; his color had definitely improved, at least.

Lady Abhasvar—until the refugees had arrived, everyone living in Anmoor had been to some degree, however attenuated, an Abhasvar. Only Piro was of the direct line and carried the name, but after the plague had swept through Anmoor, everyone who was not at least tinged with the blood had died.

And Tamasin Tealitt, sullen and resentful thirteen-year-old still utterly confounded by the healing magic that had awakened within her scant weeks before, had found that in its aftermath nobody would call her Tealitt anymore. "I'm *not* Abhasvar," she had snapped. "Most especially not *The Lady Abhasvar!*" That conversation had taken place after enduring a full week of overhearing herself referred to as such and on one memorable occasion, having been addressed so to her face by the chief (and now only) laundress.

"Very well," Shal had said, staring coldly at her mulish expression. "Tamasin, *called* Abhasvar. Is that tolerable? It pleases them to claim ownership of you. Are you so small that you'll deny them that comfort now?"

But to become Piro's wife, the *Lady Abhasvar* in truth—looked at dispassionately, it wasn't as shocking an idea as it had seemed to her three years ago when Piro had first so hesitantly proposed it. Who else had he ever gotten to know well enough to think of in that way, after all? Who else could keep him alive and healthy enough to have a real chance of siring an heir? And of course, Shal had been doing whatever he could to water and fertilize the idea in Piro's head for years, though she hadn't known that then.

She would unhesitatingly die for Piro; *living* for him, all the long years of her life, especially if he weren't even present to comfort and distract her, was an entirely different proposition. And living them in Anmoor, where summer was a barely an interruption in the endless cold, damp twilights of spring and fall–Anmoor, where there were never enough hands to do all that needed to be done day after day, month after month, year after year to keep what was left of the populace alive. And living them with *Shal*, who should never have touched her once he'd decided it was her destiny to strengthen Abhasvar' s overbred direct line with her sturdy mongrel blood—

Tamasin bent over and smoothed back Piro's bright Anmoorish hair, so different from her own unruly dark braids, and kissed him gently, just as she had when he was little. But he wasn't little, not anymore, even if her heart's eyes insisted on seeing him that way—*damn* Shal! She pulled back abruptly, wanting to damn Piro too for his unwitting complicity, but couldn't bring herself to do it. Piro could not afford to be any more damned than he already was.

After Shal had collected Piro and left for the feast, Tamasin tried to wait, to calmly stay behind in the old temple as she'd been told to do. She lasted perhaps an hour, then edged out into the corridor. It was empty; she ran fleetly down the passage to the newer parts of the keep, then crept past the kitchens to a tiny chamber, barely more than a niche, that some past untrusting Abhasvar had built on the other side of the great hall. She had to clear the cobwebs out of its squint before she could peer through it; clearly nobody had used it in some time, perhaps not since she and Piro had last spied on Shal's council gatherings, all those years ago when there had still been a council to gather.

Tamasin pressed her cheek hard against the chill stone, trying to get a better look at the high table, then recoiled involuntarily; the Riever was directly facing her, barely half the width of the hall away. He was speaking, and she strained to hear.

"—Great-Uncle doesn't even know what he's got out here, and doesn't seem to care, either—I had little trouble obtaining his permission to consolidate these wilderness territories," the Riever was saying.

"But Anmoor is no wilderness territory, my lord," came Shal's voice from somewhere outside the limited view of the squint. "Surely the Emperor never labeled us as such to you?"

"No, no, of course not! But I heard, as I was making my way up here, that fabled Anmoor had fallen silent this past decade or so! I felt it to be my duty to the Empire to investigate. Anmoor may be one of her least populous and most remote holdings, but its place in legend far outweighs all those considerations." The Riever clapped his hands together once, sharply. Into the unpleasant silence that followed, his voice rang out: "Your Grace! Isn't it well that I happened to come here just when the glorious line of Abhasvar was on the verge of dying out? I assure you, as your adopted heir, my blood will flow more strongly in your name than even yours ever could!"

The Emperor will not *be pleased,* whispered Shal's voice in Tamasin's memory, from just a few weeks before. *The Emperor almost certainly meant only to rid the Imperial court of him. Twenty years ago, when I carried the news of Piro's father's ascension there, the Emperor had far too many great-nephews and twice-removed cousins and grandsons-in-law intriguing at court for his comfort. I doubt it's any different now. Piro's great-grandfather—and yours— fought alongside the Emperor in the Indigene wars, when the Emperor was young. The Emperor was glad, very glad, when Abhasvar returned home, and he wanted them above all else to stay there.*

If this great-nephew should happen to wander all the way to Anmoor, and then should happen to disappear entirely—the Emperor is very unlikely to come looking for him.

"—keep is so well-maintained, for such an ancient holding, I nearly thought myself home again," the Riever was saying jovially. "Your servants are quite obedient, as well—who might I thank, for such efficient management?"

"My elder cousin," came Piro's voice— not weak at all, to Tamasin's intense relief. "Chief of the God's priestesses—she is resting, and meditating; she will be at the accession ceremony in the morning, if you would like to thank her then."

"I would, I would! And to assure her that with such devotion to our comforts, she'll always have a place here, no matter who is overlord."

Tamasin couldn't bear to listen to any more; Piro was as well as he ever was, and that was all she had really needed to know. She flung herself away from the squint and fled back to the old temple.

Piro returned alone a few hours later, pacing with restless energy. Tamasin did her best to project the calm demeanor of somebody who hadn't stirred outside the chamber; either it worked, or Piro was too tightly strung to notice anything amiss. "I think I know them all now," he said. He had paused beside one of the piled trunks; his fingers gripped the carven lid so tightly that the knuckles shone white. "I *think* they were all there at the feast."

"All thirty of the Riever's men?" Tamasin said, startled, and barely managed to shut her teeth over the observation that she would have expected the hall to be louder in that case—she would have made a terrible spy.

"I counted at least twenty-five—if a few were missing, then they were elsewhere—" He stopped abruptly, and their eyes met in too-perfect understanding. "I hate this," said Piro softly. "I hate that we must let him and his men run rampant through the keep." Tamasin flinched and his face hardened even more. "I made damn sure I memorized all their faces at the feast. Must we wait until dawn? For the—*accession ceremony*?" His mouth twisted on the last words.

"Shal said so." Usually the near-reverent regard in which Piro held Shal and his every word chafed on her nerves, but she found herself grateful for it now. "To increase our chances of success—sunrise, and at the place of the stones." She grimaced involuntarily. "And with me consecrated like a real live priestess. Or as close to it as we can manage." *If you can hold all those faces in your mind, all at once, no matter what else is going on—if I can keep you alive long enough to expend so much magic upon so many people—*

The telltale lines of pain and exhaustion had begun to bracket Piro's eyes and mouth, and Tamasin eventually managed to convince him to lie down. After she had let him talk himself to sleep, she slipped out the door and edged down the corridor. Shal's failure to return from the great hall was making her more and more nervous. She could hardly go wandering about the keep looking for him; the Riever knew nothing of her existence, and at this point it would be impossible to pretend, should he or his men happen across her, that it had been a mere oversight on all their parts.

She stopped at the threshold of the old temple quarters, dithering. A faint scraping noise came from behind her; she whirled around, heart pounding hard in her chest, and noticed for the first time that the door across the corridor from the high priestess's chamber was not quite shut. It was ridiculous to feel afraid; the only preternatural things in the entire keep were herself and Piro, and Anmoorish legends had nothing to say on the subject of the ghosts of priestesses past. Tamasin squared her shoulders, strode over to the door and firmly pushed it open.

The chamber beyond was much smaller than the one Piro was currently sleeping in. Shal, shirtless, filled up a good quarter of it; he was standing next to a small table and the dying remains of a hearth fire, hands full of bandages that he was clearly attempting to bind his ribs with. He looked up as the door opened, and Tamasin jerked her eyes away from his bare chest, staring fixedly at the table. "You'd better let me do that," she said, relief and irritation both serving to sharpen her voice.

He was silent for a moment; she could feel his gaze against her averted face. "All right," he said quietly. Tamasin closed the door behind her, more thoroughly than it had been before, and crossed the room to the table.

"I'm sorry they're still sore." She picked up the nearest roll of bandages. "They're not broken anymore."

"Bruising," he said, and she allowed herself the briefest of glances at his ribs— she thought she could see some mottling there, the skin darkening from the burst blood vessels beneath it. "I didn't want you to waste any more of your strength. It's only uncomfortable, nothing more."

"How stoic of you." He didn't respond to that; she didn't expect him to. She bound his chest far more efficiently that he had been going about it, though perhaps not as efficiently as she was capable of doing; she didn't usually take such care to not to brush her patient's bare flesh with her own. The second she finished she stepped back a good few paces. "There. Better, I hope."

"Yes." He paused. "And you?"

"Me? I'm fine. I could've done more for you, earlier. I'll sleep a little. I'll need to be up again at least an hour before you and Piro anyway." She didn't really want to ask, but she had to. "Will anyone be able to help me with the preparations?" *Untraumatized, unwounded...?* She braced herself for the answer.

After several excruciating seconds, Shal said, "I don't know yet."

"Ah." There wasn't much else to say to that. The silence that fell between them was no more uncomfortable than usual. She started to turn away from him, then stopped as his fingers gripped her wrist.

She couldn't remember the last time he had touched her voluntarily, of his own accord—or rather she *could*, but he had made a point of not doing so, even in passing, since then. She was startled into looking up at his face, and the sight of it surprised her even more—he looked ravaged, was the only way she could think to describe it. *Him!* "You love him," said Shal, and either exhaustion or the exigency of the moment had roughened his voice, violating its usual cool control. "Why won't you save Abhasvar?"

Shock quickly gave way to outrage. "I *am* helping save it, supposedly! First thing in the morning—"

"And afterwards?"

Her laugh was short and sharp. "You think there'll be one?"

"There may be." Tamasin opened her mouth, then closed it. There were twenty answers to that, each more incoherent than the last, all boiling over with emotion. "The princess of Anmoor can do whatever she pleases," Shal continued in a low voice. Tamasin went rigid. "She can have whomever she pleases, once she's done her duty by Abhasvar—"

"My *God*, what you think of me!" Tamasin wrenched her wrist from his grasp. Her cheeks felt like they were on fire, skin stretched tight as a drum. "Even when I *thought* I wanted you—"

"I want Abhasvar to live," said Shal, meeting her eyes without any evidence of shame or self-doubt—was he even capable of those emotions? "It can, through you. And you do love him."

"Of course I love him," she said. "He always loved me, even when I was nobody and nothing. I could even do what you're asking—*not* the part where I have *whomever I please*—" She stopped; her voice had begun to shake. After a deep breath, she continued, more calmly, "But none of that matters now, does it? None of us may even be alive by this time tomorrow."

"But we may be," he said. "And if we are, Tamasin—please." His jaw was so tight that the muscles twitched under his cheekbones. "Please. It would make Piro very happy—does that move you, at least?"

And what about me? she wanted to shout at him. *What about* my *happiness?* —but that argument would never move Shal. He never considered his own happiness, after all—well, he had once, if *happiness* was the proper word for what had happened between them all those years ago. *She* had been happy, at least— but she'd been a fool. Tamasin did not enjoy being a fool. "I've said I'll consider it," she said flatly. "I've said so to Piro." Shal's eyes widened. "I'm surprised he didn't tell you. He's asked me to marry him at summer solstice." Unwilling to even look at him any longer, Tamasin turned her back on him and stalked towards the door. "Try to get a little sleep," she said, over her shoulder. "I'm going to do the same. Then find someone to help me get ready before sunrise."

Later, Tamasin was never sure if she had slept—she thought she must at least have dozed off, sitting on the floor beside Piro's bed, because the sound of the door opening startled her fully awake. She lifted her head from the side of the mattress, careful not to jostle the still-sleeping Piro as Anbeg, once chief laundress and now Tamasin's second in everything else domestic in the keep as well, poked her head into the chamber. Tamasin rose creakily to her feet and padded to the door and out into the corridor.

Anbeg, her arms piled high with cloth and satchels, led her to the door across the corridor behind which Shal had been, earlier. Tamasin eyed it as if it were a striking snake, but Anbeg simply nudged it open with her hip and continued inside without pause. Tamasin followed her, closing and barring the door behind them. Shal had at least built the fire up before he left—the little room was brightly lit now, and almost uncomfortably warm.

Anbeg crossed the floor to the small table and set her burdens down carefully, then turned to face Tamasin. She didn't look any the worse for wear—but she wasn't young; perhaps she'd been spared the attentions of the Riever and his men. "My lady," said Anbeg sturdily.

Tamasin sighed. Anbeg had always been the most resistant to simply addressing her as *Tamasin*. "Do you know what to do? Because I don't, not really."

"I was an acolyte, once," said Anbeg. At Tamasin's startled look, she cracked a small, dry smile. "Wouldn't think it, would you, my lady? But I had the blood. Obviously. It never blossomed, though." She turned away and busied herself opening the satchels and spreading their contents out across the tables—sticks of color, small capped ceramic pots, a handful of golden vials, brushes and combs. Tamasin idly fingered the billowing piles of cloth—beneath the topmost, pure white layer were several more, heavily embroidered and alternating purple and black.

"Black?" Tamasin asked, plucking up an edge to show Anbeg.

"It's still just the purple—if you concentrate the dye enough, you get black," said Anbeg. "We used to sell a lot of it, the black and purple cloth, when traders came through the mountains. They didn't know that either." The small, dry smile made a reappearance. "They thought it was magic. They gave us good coin for it."

"Useful," said Tamasin, with a faint smile of her own. No traders had visited Anmoor since the plague—in fact, nobody at all had until now, other than the Emperor's tax collector once a year, and he never came further in than the border garrison at the southern pass. It had been a challenge to make the garrison actually appear manned for those visits—but they had been recovering. They *had*.

There was no point in dwelling on that now. "Should I change into it?" Hoping she *could*—she had no idea how it was put together, and the stained-glass frescoes in the old temple depicting the priestesses in full regalia, while long on beauty, were short on fine details.

"No. We'll do the rest first." *The rest* turned out to be the paints and powders and brushes—lacking a chair, Tamasin alternately stood and knelt as Anbeg ordered her to—a role reversal for both of them, but if Anbeg found it uncomfortable or unnerving, she gave no sign of either.

Tamasin found Anbeg's dispassionate demeanor a relief when it came time to strip off her robe and the shift beneath. "Three vials," Anbeg murmured, "containing the fluid of the God's own flesh—tears, saliva, sweat. Close your eyes, my lady." Tamasin did, and felt something cool trickle down her scalp, then between her breasts, then down the small of her back. "Now stand."

Tamasin's feet had begun itching from standing motionless for so long by the time Anbeg had finished wrapping her in the complex, butter-soft folds of cloth. The unconfined weight of her hair, a state it was almost never in, unnerved her; she could feel it slithering across her shoulder blades and swinging against her elbows as she turned around to face Anbeg.

Anbeg backed slowly away from her, expressionless. That expressionlessness was more than Anbeg's usual stoicism. "What?" Tamasin burst out finally.

"I haven't seen a true priestess in an awfully long time, my lady," said Anbeg. Her voice was hoarse in the thick silence that had fallen.

"The hair ruins the whole thing, I expect," said Tamasin, trying for breeziness.

But Anbeg shook her head and backed up a few more steps. "The young prince will do what he must," she said softly, "just as his grandfather did in his day, when the Wolfclans came across the mountains to raid us. The prince's mother and aunt were only girls then, but they were consecrated true priestesses and healed him afterward, my father told me. He was there, and saw it with his own eyes."

"What else did your father say about it?" Tamasin's voice was harsher than she meant it to be. "About—Piro's grandfather, and what he did? What was it—" She trailed off.

Anbeg pinched her lips together. "He wouldn't tell that part," she said finally. "He didn't want to talk about it. The prince's grandfather lived, and so did most of his men, and the raiders all died. That's enough to know."

After bidding Anbeg farewell, Tamasin slipped out of the keep. The Riever had posted no guards, and indeed, why should he have? He and his men were the only things that menaced the keep. It was dark enough to make following the path a bit tricky, but Tamasin knew the way—she and Piro had sneaked out here often enough when Shal had imagined them hard at work in the nursery schoolroom instead.

To most of the Anmoorish, this was a sacred place; to Tamasin, even after the magic had wakened in her, it had never felt any different from anywhere else. The standing stones were certainly impressive, each one twice her height and several times her breadth, with a blackened sconce atop each where generations of mage-princes had summoned orblights for their priestesses' supplicants. She spared them barely a glance before dropping to her knees in the soft grass. Even through her cloak, and the ceremonial robes beneath it, the ground was icy, as was the breeze that wafted through the gaps between the stones. She was glad of it; she thought she would be sweating like a pig otherwise, from the layers of cloth swaddling her and her own fear.

She had only just beaten them out here —bare moments later, she heard them approaching. The Riever's voice rang out, bright and mocking; Shal's low tones answered, unintelligibly, then Piro's lighter ones. When she was sure they could all see her, she rose as gracefully to her feet as she could, keeping herself swathed in the cloak's heavy folds.

The long grass rustled as the men pushed their way through it. Two of the Riever's men gripped Shal's arms, shackled in front of him; his ankles were chained barely a foot apart and a fresh bruise was swelling his jaw. Piro stood beside the Riever, who clearly felt his mere presence was sufficient restraint for the prince of Anmoor. Piro looked well—more than well—his eyes were shining, and it amazed her that the Riever didn't notice, or didn't care if he did.

"Priestess," said Piro, his voice clear and bright in the sharp dawn air. "Please begin the ceremony."

Tamasin bowed her head in what she hoped was a ceremonial fashion, then whipped her cloak off. She'd practiced that maneuver ten or fifteen times back in the chamber, until she could do it without tangling it up in either her legs or her hair, and it spilled back flawlessly off her shoulders to puddle at her feet. The rising sun caught her robes and lit the metallic embroidery to orange-gold; she shone in the light, and the men all stared at her, transfixed.

"Why, where were you keeping this one?" cried the Riever. He looked her up and down, ostentatiously. "This can't be your *elder* cousin! Does she come with the crown?"

Piro gazed at her for a long moment, his eyes serious and steady on her face. "I hope she does," he said. "Priestess. Please begin."

"Your Grace," said Tamasin. Her voice was a little choked; she swallowed as surreptitiously as she could and said, more strongly, "Do you choose, at this break of day, to relinquish your hold on the princedom of Anmoor, to pass on all honors and birthrights to your chosen heir?" Shal had come up with the wording. It had sounded a lot more impressive when he had said it, especially with the echo that had been imparted by the surrounding stone walls of the keep; the emptiness of the sky all around them swallowed her own voice whole.

"I do," said Piro.

"Then, prince and prince-to-be, come to me, and"—for an eternal, awful second she blanked on what she was supposed to say next—"receive the gifts of the God!" Tamasin raised her hands and spat on both palms, the only genuine part of the entire thing, then held them out; the Riever looked faintly revolted. But he walked forward with Piro and clasped her hand anyway—his was far larger and rougher than Piro's familiar palm. The Riever squeezed then, brutally hard, but she was too keyed up to react. The sky was darkening in her sight, a reversal of the sunrise, as Piro's magic swelled against her flesh.

There had been no way to practice this; they had both been equally unwilling to do so on anyone else, Anmoorish or refugee. It would either work, or it wouldn't. Tamasin thought distantly under the onslaught of Piro's magic that *something* was going to work—she had never felt anything quite like this. She thought she heard shouting, and a muffled clang of steel on steel, but she could do nothing about any of it.

A man screamed, high and hoarse as a boy, and the Riever's hand wrenched itself from her loose grasp. Piro staggered against her and she groped for his other hand, found it and squeezed it tightly in hers. Piro's magic surged again and finally, her own healing magic rose to meet it—that at least was familiar, the shuddering heat flooding her body and surging down her arms to his hands gripping hers.

Light boiled around them. Her eyes were working again, and everything was brilliant, eerie green; the orblights atop each standing stone had ignited. The Riever had fallen to his knees beside Shal, his fists buried in his own heavy black hair. The screams were his; his men had staggered back, faces bleached and working in the emerald haze.

The Riever's screams turned into guttural, mindless ululations—one of his men broke and fled, achieving five or six strides before he fell to own knees, clutching his head. The other wrenched his sword clumsily from its scabbard and swung it sideways at Shal, who rolled away unscathed. The man dropped his sword, fingers ripping at his own cheeks as he toppled sideways. *What about the others?* she said, or thought she said— could Piro hear her over the dying howls of the Riever's men?

It appeared he could; his lips were in her hair and his voice vibrated through her skull. *The same thing's happening all throughout the keep; our people are running, hiding in the old temple passages and the storerooms.* And they were safe from the withering—that was what Shal had called it, what his old texts and diaries had named it, what had induced the then-youthful Emperor of Un to do everything but outright exile his Abhasvar vassals after he'd seen them make war.

Tamasin could feel it now, like the roaring of a winter storm muffled by the keep's thick stone walls—but the Anmoorish and the refugees were all safe behind the walls of Piro's will. He was controlling the withering, forcing its life-draining power through the narrowest of channels: *only the Riever and the men who serve him,* these *faces, only them, only—*

The Riever had stopped screaming; his body was twitching and his empty eyes were staring at her and Piro, but no more sounds emerged from his gaping mouth. *Should I be horrified?* Tamasin looked past the Riever, at the gobbling, convulsing remains of his men, and couldn't bring herself to even try to be. Piro's arms tightened against hers and she burrowed in closer, fiercely glad that they were dead and that Piro was alive, and loving him so much it hurt.

I love you too, he whispered. *I've always loved you.* She could hardly tell where Piro left off and she began, in the shared maelstrom of their magic; she didn't resist when he turned her fully around to face him and let go of one of her hands to cup her chin in his palm, tilting her head back. Her eyes closed as Piro's mouth gently covered hers. A different sort of heat intruded, prickling across her flesh, and Piro's body pressed harder against hers as her lips parted beneath his. She had been a woman grown for five years, had grimly struggled alone against the desires of one for most of that time, and her body knew what it wanted now regardless of who was providing it.

Suddenly every muscle in Piro's body locked—Tamasin jerked her mouth away from Piro's and staggered back, only his hand still clenched in hers keeping her by his side. That was all the warning she had before the withering, as soulless and terrible as a hundredweight of dead stone, came surging back into him. Piro screamed, a terrible harsh cry, and because she was still utterly entangled in him she felt her *(his)* mind begin to come apart at the seams, fragmenting under that hideous grinding pressure.

When a priestess recalls her magic to herself after healing, it's greatly weakened, having poured itself into her supplicants, Shal had said to Piro and Tamasin, that night weeks ago when they had all finally realized the magnitude of the danger they were in. *Yet what little is left of it restores her, heals* her *just as it healed* them, *because that is its most basic nature. When a mage-prince recalls the withering to himself, it's swollen to bursting with the life force of all its victims, and it will do its damnedest to kill him just as it killed them, because that's its most basic nature. Those stolen lives must be drained from the withering until it is weak enough that he can control it, and banish it once more.*

Tamasin had hoped fervently that this use of her magic would come to her as easily as the healing did, and it *was* easy, at first. As she determinedly siphoned the withering's tidal wave of life force away, it sprinted through her veins like sunlight, bright and ephemeral, swelling her inner reservoir of magic. Piro's hand in hers slowly began to relax. She drained it, and drained it, and ignored the faint, growing ache in her head and belly. She could heal herself as well as she could any other Abhasvar; if she took a little damage now, what of it? A *little* damage—but the ache persisted, and deepened, and she gritted her teeth through it and thought *I can heal a* lot *of damage, too—just let me finish, damn you!*

But the priestesses, she thought suddenly, *in the frescoes in the old temple*—the high priestess with her hands in the mage-prince's and all the lesser priestesses standing around them in a circle with their own hands clasped together, waiting...waiting for the head priestess to tire, each to take her place in turn and drain the withering. But Tamasin had no other priestesses to call upon, and now the ache could no longer truly be called an *ache*. It was a rock of agony in her stomach and behind her eyes, radiating outward until she couldn't even see the standing stones and the slumped bodies and Shal anymore—*Shal!*

Shal had no magic of his own, but he was Abhasvar and that might be enough. Blindly she spat on her free hand and thrust it out, praying that Shal was still conscious and could possibly figure out what she needed him to do in time.

Fingers grasped hers, strong and hard, and suddenly Shal was *with* them in the tumult of their shared sorcery. The crushing weight of the life force still pouring out from the withering into her abruptly shifted, the reduction of the accompanying pain such a relief that she gasped aloud as her vision swam back into focus. For one long, perfect moment the three of them were balanced against the withering and then it was shrinking, rolling back like a storm front in reverse. In its wake the three-way bond of magic between Tamasin, Piro, and Shal snapped into focus and to her horror, she saw that Piro had clearly sustained more than a *little* damage himself, his mind wavering and half-lost. And Shal—his pale hazel eyes, barely inches from her face, were locked on hers—and she could *feel* it, feel the sullen heat of his desire for her, ruthlessly suppressed by his duty to Abhasvar but never entirely eradicated. A searing memory boiled up between the two of them, the *three* of them—her own face, eyes shut tight, neck arched back, sweat shining on her bare breasts and the feel of herself around him, slick and tight and hot—

Both Tamasin and Piro recoiled, Piro's reaction so intense he actually took a step backward, pulling Tamasin along with him. Shock and betrayal ripped into the link between them all like jagged spears—and then, horribly, the withering spilled out of Piro in a sudden scalding torrent towards Shal. Shal jerked like a marionette, the hopelessly tangled shackles and chains that were still wrapped around his arms and legs shrieking as they grated together.

Tamasin opened her mouth to scream, at Piro or Shal she hardly knew, but before she could do more than take a single breath, the withering was upon her as well. A terrible lassitude replaced all her own magic so utterly that for an instant she thought she had simply died; her legs buckled, collapsing her into a heap on the ground, the weight of her falling body wrenching her hand from Piro's grasp. A vast, cool wind filled her head, sweeping everything that made her Tamasin away with it. She rolled onto her back with the last of her strength and found herself staring up into Piro's eyes, eyes glaring with the sickly green radiance of the orblights.

Piro's mouth was open, his lips forming her name but she couldn't hear anything except a dull, rhythmic thudding. The last thing she saw, before the withering swallowed her utterly in its infinite empty darkness, was Piro's face contorted into a rictus of agony and determination.

Tamasin tightened the straps on her old haversack, kept from that long-ago journey to Anmoor, then set it down in the pile of what was left of her belongings at the end of her bed. When she thought about carrying all of it, on foot for weeks or even months, the pile looked enormous, but when she thought about surviving on its contents, it looked pathetically tiny instead.

The door to her bedchamber creaked open. *I should have somebody oil that*, she thought, then realized how ridiculous the thought was—the state of any and all door hinges throughout the keep would henceforth be someone else's problem. She looked up; Shal stood there, gazing expressionlessly at her. Well, he could hardly be surprised, unless he hadn't taken seriously any of her twenty recent declarations on the subject of leaving.

But his staring nettled her. "Your Grace," she said evenly. His lips tightened, then he came in and closed the door behind him. His eyes were on her hair, and when his nostrils flared she said, "Yes, I burned it after I cut it all off." The acrid stench still lingered around the hearth.

"Why?" he asked.

"Why did I cut it all off, or why did I burn it?"

"Both."

"I cut it off because it would be a disaster to take care of on the road, and I burned it because—" The sight of it after she had sawed it off, piled on her mattress in a mass of tangled dark curls, had made her cry, and she had shoved it blindly into the fire to stop that bitter flood of tears. "Because why not?"

"Don't go," he said, and all her insouciance was silenced, just like that. His face was drawn—thinner, and the usually firm flesh of his cheeks and jaw sagged a little. "You're needed here."

"Not anymore," she said, and her voice was harsh and grating in her own ears.

"People still fall ill—"

"They'll live! They can't catch the plague twice, and they'll survive anything else!"

"—and suffer injuries, and bear children—"

"*I don't care.*" Her eyes were filling again, *damn* him! Tamasin dug her nails into her palms, harder and harder until the pain drove the tears back into abeyance. "That's not true," she said, as mildly as she could once she was sure she could control her voice. "I do care. But I need to leave."

"Where will you go?"

She had thought long and hard about that. "Nebra had a college of physicians and midwives," she said finally. "People used to come from all over the Empire to visit it. I may try to win a place there." She shrugged irritably. "I realize that very few, if any, of my future patients could benefit from my...*special* gifts, but I've delivered enough babies in the past ten years to have acquired a respectable amount of mundane skill as well."

"I've never been able to touch the magic," he said abruptly. "I've only ever even felt it that once. When—"

Tamasin flinched, then said thinly, "I'm surprised that you think it needs to be said aloud, here, between us, that this is all my fault. But since it *is*—"

"You should know better than that. You *do* know better than that."

"There!" she said, and the venom in her voice surprised even her. "*That's* you. I was starting to wonder if you'd somehow replaced yourself with someone else, these past few weeks—"

"The people still accept you," he said, calm again. "They've accepted you for many years. Even loved you." Tamasin stiffened. "Not just Piro. And nobody blames you for his death."

She wanted to scream at him for speaking of love, and Piro, and death all at once, in his even, measured tones—but she didn't; she counted her heartbeats until the urge to do so faded. The last part might even have been true; she had been unconscious for three days after the deaths of the Riever and all his men. It might simply have seemed to everyone else that both she and Piro had tried to sacrifice their lives to save Anmoor, and only she had been strong enough to recover from it; Piro's steadily worsening health had hardly been a secret. But she didn't need anyone else's blame to validate her own.

"I suppose you feel you must do this, because now they're yours," she said flatly. "All Anmoor is yours now by right, and who else is there to help you care for it? As you say, *you're* magicless." He didn't react to that; with a sigh, she gave up on further provocation and said, wearily, "But I *am* proof that the magic can manifest where you'd least expect it. Marry another Abhasvar and have ten children. You might be surprised."

He gazed at her for a long moment; she looked away. "You're hardly exiled," she heard him say. "If you ever want to return, you'll be welcomed. Assuming you survive."

"*Thank* you," she said briskly. "Always the voice of comfort and cheer! None of the refugees are staying either, you know —their homes are at least possibly reclaimable, now that the Riever and his men are gone, and Anmoor has turned out to be a little too much like the old tales made it out. They've offered to let me travel with them, so my chances of survival, at least until I reach the lowlands, really aren't that terrible—"

"All right," he said tonelessly. The silence that fell between them was distinctly sticky. "Goodbye, Tamasin."

She waited until she was sure he was gone before she moved, bending down to pick up her haversack, her belts and bags and cloak. The refugees were all bedding down in the hall tonight, with their bundles and boxes, ready to move out at the first light of day; she would join them, so there would be no delay in leaving and no chance they'd leave without her. She swept one last look around at the room that had been hers since she'd first come to Anmoor so many years ago, but she didn't feel anything for it. Piro was dead, and this room held nothing of his presence anymore.

She tried anyway. "Goodbye, Piro," she whispered. But nothing answered back; the room was silent except for the faint hissing of the dying coals in the hearth. Tamasin, called Abhasvar, turned on her heel and strode out the door, not bothering to close it behind her.

"See Lisa Short's story "The Season of Withering" online at Metaphorosis.
If you liked it, leave a comment. Authors love that!

*Remember to subscribe to our e-mail updates so
   you'll know when new stories are posted."*

About the story

I have the (probably peculiar) lifelong habit of
making up bedtime stories and telling them to myself
when I'm having trouble getting to sleep at night. A lot
of the stories I end up writing have this exercise as
their inspirational mechanism, and this particular one
definitely originated as a "bedtime story." I didn't get
much past the opening scene (I usually don't, because
I fall asleep at that point!) but that scene, and the four
main actors in it, were so vividly realized that I really
couldn't wait to explore how they had all gotten there,
why that scene was unfolding the way it was, and
what was going to happen to them next.

A question for the author

Q: What is your favorite story?

A: My favorite stories have always been of the "hero
who overcomes childhood/adolescent adversity
because they're so smart and hard-working" variety—
with the caveat that it isn't presented as some kind of
paean to capitalism and/or Social Darwinism. My very
favorites are ones where the hero is (a) a heroine and
(b) the adversity doesn't consist solely or even mostly
of sexual trauma (because that has been done to
death).

About the author

Lisa Short is a Texas-born, Kansas-bred writer of fantasy and science fiction. She has an honorable discharge from the United States Army, a degree in chemical engineering, and twenty years' experience as a professional engineer. She recently started a blog for her writing and is working on her first novel. She currently lives in Maryland with her husband, two youngest children, father-in-law and cats.

lisashortwrites.blogspot.com, @Lisa_K_Short

Super

Yume Kitasei

The last time Jack Wu jumped off a building, he nearly lost an arm clipping the fire escape. Something wrong with his takeoff. Maybe it took a few seconds longer to catch an upstream or something, he didn't know. God, it had hurt like hell.

But then he was up in the arms of the grey sky again, his hands out in front of him in the night above the city, looking for trouble.

When he got home, his arm still throbbed, and he was bickering with his back. He went straight to the fridge for the frozen peas to defrost against his lower vertebrae. He'd forgotten his phone by the sink, and there was a message from Penelope. His heart stuttered. Was something wrong with the kid? That had been his paralyzing fear since the day Sebastian was born. Something happening to Sebastian, Jack not there to save him.

"Calm down," Penelope said when she picked up. She could tell he had already worked himself into a circus again. "We're completely fine. The house isn't burning down. Listen, I've got to go out of town for a conference. So you need to take Sebastian for a week. And don't tell me you're too busy. I make it work every day; you can make it work for a week."

He removed the peas from his back and flexed experimentally, grimaced at the stab of pain. He wanted to want to say yes, but even the anticipation exhausted him. He exhaled slowly over the sink and said: "I'd love to take Sebastian."

It rained buckets that night. Right as he was sinking into the deepness of sleep that comes with the reassuring percussion of rain on the window, Jack got a call about a missing child, last seen being swallowed by the maw of a blue Volvo. He went out, but it took him half an hour to get into the sky. By the time he did, his old sneakers were soaked through, and he regretted not changing out of his pajamas.

It was an evil kind of dark and nearly impossible to see a thing through the downpour. Then lightning shattered the sky, and in between the cracks of it, he spotted a flash of metallic blue. The license plate was a match. Down he went and kicked open the door. It was midnight, and the child sat in a dirty diaper, eating applesauce with a broken spoon. Jack tied up the kidnapper, changed the diaper, called the cops.

When they came, he had to beg a ride, because he couldn't feel the air between his cold, numb fingers. He stretched for it, tried to rise, but nothing: a wet match that couldn't scrape a light.

"You all right, Jack?" one of the cops asked.

"Sure," said Jack. "Just tired." And he felt that way to his bones.

Sebastian arrived with a backpack and a runny nose. Penelope handed him a heavy suitcase.

"Oh," said Jack. "I'd been looking for that."

"It's mine," she said.

Jack's phone pinged, and he glanced at it. Cat in a tree. *Get your own goddamned cat*, he thought. *I'm with my son.*

He squatted down and held out his arms. The boy shrank back a moment behind his mom's thigh, and Jack's heart squeezed from the betrayal. It had only been a year since Penelope asked him to move out. He still saw Sebastian as often as he could. Which was not enough.

The first three years of Sebastian's life, he'd really tried to do it all: he'd do Sebastian's night feed while Penelope slept, then put Sebastian down, jump out the window, answer a cry for help, get back in time for breakfast. Penelope had asked him to cut back, be more present. "Last I checked, flying didn't mean you can be two places at once. Or not sleep," she said. And invincibility didn't mean Sebastian's shrill wail didn't make him hurt inside, his pulse stampede. He could hear it from a mile away. Each time, he thought something unspeakable had happened. He would abandon the job and fly right back, only to find Sebastian had merely dropped a spoon on the floor. He had tried, he really had.

"Say hi to Daddy," Penelope said.

"No," said Sebastian and turned his face away.

"He's just shy these days," said Penelope. "Sebastian, that's not very nice."

"I don't want to stay here," said Sebastian, and each word was like a bullet hitting Jack's chest.

Later, after she left, Sebastian perked up a little bit, and Jack couldn't remember why he ever thought this was hard. They watched cartoons on the big, sagging couch, and Sebastian put his dirty feet up on Jack's lap, until Jack tickled them, and Sebastian laughed and laughed and then kicked him in the jaw.

"Ow," said Jack.

Sebastian buried his head immediately in a couch arm, bracing for a barrage of harsh words to follow, because his dad never understood that you could do a thing you didn't mean. It was always Sebastian, *don't,* Sebastian, *stop it now,*

Sebastian, *you're in big trouble mister.* Jack read all this in the bracket of his son's shoulders, and he felt like crying himself.

His phone rang. He didn't answer it. Three times, he almost called them back. But didn't.

The Fire Department texted him about a three-alarm fire all the way across town. A wave of cold anxiety washed over him, and he took a breath. *Sorry,* he responded. *I have my son this week.*

"Come on, you," he said to Sebastian. "Let's go to the playground." And he hauled Sebastian over his shoulder like a sack of potatoes, and Sebastian howled and pounded his back with his fists and pretended to be outraged. Jack growled, declared himself a big, blue monster, and threatened to eat him up.

As they walked to the playground, Sebastian said, "Can't we fly, Daddy?"

"I don't think so, kiddo. Sorry." He massaged his arm, thinking about how he'd gone for a run that morning, and he'd sprinted and jumped and nearly faceplanted on the pavement after missing the sky. He never missed the sky. "I think I'm getting too old."

"But I want to," said Sebastian, beginning to sniffle.

"I know, sweetie," he said. "Me too." But what he really wanted was to lie down right there on the concrete and let the sun soak through his skin, he was that empty.

He didn't blame Penelope. She had started making plans without him, hiring strangers to babysit their son. He had said, *but I'm here. But you're not*, she'd replied. They negotiated. He stopped taking calls on Saturdays. He gave Penelope his phone as a hostage, so nobody could even reach him. The city complained about that. "Saturday is Death Day" said one particularly annoying headline, all because the rate of homicides and accidental casualties had ticked up for Saturdays. Marginally.

"It's not even statistically significant," said Penelope, pulling off her reading glasses so she could rub her eyes. She was an economist and knew these things.

"It's my fault," he said. He went and threw up in the toilet. He looked in the mirror and saw there was silver in his black hair. He hadn't told Penelope how he'd pulled a muscle taking off earlier, and he remembered aging had come the same way for his mother, who had ignored it until the end, even after she broke a hip coming down from the sky.

"Feel better?" Penelope had asked.

"No."

She'd picked up Sebastian, kissed him on his nose, helped him pick out a new crayon. She'd given up for the day on making progress with her research. Didn't look up when he went to her jewelry box where she kept his phone. And when he came home again, she'd said: maybe it's better we don't do this anymore.

He'd tried to argue. He cried. She cried. (Sebastian cried too, with his ambulance wail.)

"I'm sorry," Jack said.

"And yet," she said.

She was kinder than she needed to be. If only he hadn't felt so relieved. Later, that was what he hated most about himself.

Sebastian was even more of a handful now. He was two hands full. He vibrated with the energy of ten thousand bees. Not his fault, of course. It was Jack's fault. He shouldn't have bought Sebastian the ice cream cone. Penelope had, in fact, warned him about sugar, but how could Jack have predicted how off the wall Sebastian would be? Sebastian did *not* want to go to bed. He did *not* want to eat the takeout Jack ordered specially for him. He did *not* want to take a bath. He did *not* want to call Mommy. He did *not* want to calm down. NO! NO! NO! NO! NO! NO! NO! NO! NO! NO! NO! NO! NO! NO!

And Jack had been trying all afternoon to recapture Sebastian's love, to be gentle, to be patient, to be the Best Dad on Earth. He sat on the couch and put his head in his hands while Sebastian threw his legos at the wall and hollered at the top of his lungs.

"Please," Jack said. "Please don't shout." A stormfront was building in his temples, and his back hurt again from picking Sebastian up all day.

The boy was all carbonation, vigorously shaken, fizzing out through his perforated seams. If only Jack could get him to sit down. *I can't do this,* he thought. *But I have to. I have to be the best for him.* He could feel the surface of his temper begin to bubble up inside, reach one hundred degrees even as he struggled against it.

His phone rang. It rang again. He picked it up and threw it across the coffee table.

"Boogerface!" said Sebastian, as he passed Jack in his march around and around the couch, battering its cushions with the abused cover of his picture book.

Jack went and got the phone. Thirteen messages.

Jack, where are you?

ASAP

"Butthead!" Sebastian said.

need your help

city needs

bus crash

"I hate you!" Sebastian said.

traffic signal out

school

gunfight

jumper

brake problems

missing

dead

please

"Hey!" said Sebastian, with his hands on his hips, practically shouting in Jack's ear. "I'm talking to you! Did you hear me?"

"SHUT UP!" Jack regretted the words even as they were coming out of his mouth.

"No, *you* shut up!" And then Sebastian immediately began to sob like the world was ending.

"I'm sorry," said Jack. He tried to hug his son, but Sebastian ran to his room and slammed the door.

Jack got up off the floor and went to get the frozen peas from the kitchen.

He sighed gratefully as the cold touched his skin.

Sebastian came stomping back in. "Hey! Poop emoji!"

And then when Jack didn't respond, Sebastian kicked the leg of the kitchen table so the utensils in the drawer rattled. "I'm *talking* to you!"

Jack waited, sipping his breaths. *This time I'll be better. I'll understand.*

Then Sebastian slammed into him full-tilt and wrapped his arms around Jack's legs. He turned his little face up to Jack. There was dirt on his nose, and his eyelashes were sticky with tears. "Why won't you play with me?" he asked.

"I wish you wouldn't shout," said Jack, sliding down to sit with his back to the cabinet and wrap his arms around his son like a seatbelt.

"I'm sorry."

"Me too."

Jack pressed his face into the boy's hair and smelled the grass and the sunshine and four year old sweat from a day of running around, and he thought, if he could just bottle this moment, right now, then he wouldn't need to fly anyway.

They went to the diner and ordered hash browns, just hash browns, because that was all Sebastian wanted. Sebastian was well-behaved until the second half of the meal. It was like a switch was flipped. He was angry, he was sullen. He would not talk or look at Jack.

"Kids," said the waitress sympathetically. "It's just that age, you know."

"I know."

"Hey, don't I know you from somewhere?" she asked.

"Don't think so," said Jack. He did know her. He'd rescued her half-naked from the back of a car, bloody and only semi-conscious. He didn't want her to remember that. So he left a good tip and took Sebastian home.

"What about the zoo?" asked Sebastian.

"Tomorrow," said Jack.

"You have to work?"

He saw Sebastian's lower lip begin to tremble, so he scooped him up and held him close. "I love you, okay?" He said this again, but he felt like there was no way to say it in a way the boy would understand.

Sebastian fell asleep in his arms.

In his back pocket, he could hear his phone ringing, again and again, miniscule grappling hooks piercing his skin. He thought he should answer it. He didn't.

Jack took a hop-skip and tried to fly. The sky wouldn't take him. He tried again.

"Shit," he said.

He hailed a cab instead.

"Hey," said the driver. "Aren't you–"

"Shh," said Jack, putting his fingers to his lips. He pointed to his son, snuggled against him.

After, the driver wouldn't take his money. "I never knew you took cabs," he said, shaking his head. A big goofy grin was plastered across his face from ear to ear. He left Jack standing on the street with his wallet out.

Detective Greene was waiting for him on the stoop.

"Chief thought maybe something got you," said the Detective.

"Daddy?" said Sebastian, waking up. "Can you carry me upstairs?"

"Okay," said Jack, even though his arms felt like lead.

"We called you a bunch of times. Did you lose your phone?"

"No," said Jack. "I have my son for the week."

"Right," said Detective Greene.

Jack began to take the stairs. He never took the stairs; he usually went straight through the window.

"Everything all right with you?"

"I'm doing fine. Cut myself with the knife last night making chili, though." He showed the detective his hand.

"What are you wearing a bandage for?"

"I told you, I cut myself."

"I thought you didn't bleed."

"I'm forty-five," said Jack. Detective Greene shook his head like this was impossible. "I'm not going to be around forever, you know. You've got to learn how to deal with your own problems."

Jack kept on climbing and left the detective at the bottom. There were seventy-three stairs, enough to suck the wind out of him.

"Good night, Daddy," said Sebastian, tucking his head into Jack's neck. And even though Jack's legs and arms burned, he thought he could continue standing there, holding his son, until the moon crashed into the sea.

They played checkers in the park. They went to a movie. He taught Sebastian how to ride a skateboard (carefully, clutching his hand all the while).

He dreaded Friday, when Penelope would come home, and he would have to give the boy back. But also, he counted the minutes until the little tyrant would have someone else to boss around.

"I never appreciated how patient you were," Jack told her when she called to check in.

"It's not patience. It's endurance," she said.

"You're superhuman," he said.

"Don't be silly. You of all people."

He didn't tell her that he'd tried to fly one night while Sebastian was asleep. Someone had called him about a situation involving a woman and her daughter and a boyfriend with a gun. He couldn't just plug his ears and look away, could he? He had to go. That's what he thought. He opened the window and spread his arms and willed himself to float. Nada. So he ran all the way down the stairs and borrowed the neighbor's bike. The cops beat him there. The woman was wounded, but she and her daughter were alive. Turned out, they didn't need Jack after all.

When he got back, Sebastian was curled up on the couch, clutching Penguin. He had been crying a long time and had peed on the couch, a big wet patch, the shape of his abandonment stained into the fabric.

"Where did you go, Daddy?" Sebastian asked. "I was scared."

And Jack felt like he was drowning in his mistake. If something had happened—

He wrapped Sebastian up in his arms and said again and again: "I'm sorry, I'm sorry," and knew it would never be enough.

The last night, Jack took Sebastian to a baseball game downtown. They sat in the cheap seats right beneath the sky and ate peanuts and yelled when the home team did well and yelled when they didn't. Even though Sebastian had insisted he didn't want to go, he enjoyed himself immensely, and when it was done, he asked when they could go again.

As they walked to catch the bus, a dissonant chorus of sirens passed them, headed down Fourth Avenue.

Sebastian watched them go with his ears covered. Then he swung his plastic inflatable bat and hop-skipped down the sidewalk. And for a moment, just a moment, he seemed to float in the air. Jack saw it, and his breath caught in his throat.

Then Sebastian's feet touched the ground again, and he stumbled a little and giggled. "I tripped. Oopsie."

"Oopsie," Jack agreed. He grabbed Sebastian's hand tight.

His phone rang, and Sebastian put his thumb in his mouth and watched him answer it.

It was the Chief of Police, who hadn't called him in days.

"Jack. I know you've got your kid with you right now, and you're going through an existential fucking crisis, but this is important. There's a bomb downtown in a bank, and my guys are saying it could take out multiple buildings."

A crowd of people came running. There was a falafel cart guy carrying his spatula and people in suits and a woman limping along on a broken high heel. And all around the air was like the inside of a balloon about to burst.

"Run," someone told him as she passed.

"Jack?" said the Chief.

"You have a bomb squad," Jack said.

"C'mon Jack, please. Don't make me beg here."

Sebastian looked up at him with big eyes. He swung the plastic bat at Jack's knee, and Jack barely felt it. He felt better than he'd felt in a long time.

"Where is it?" Jack asked.

"By the Credit Union at Fourth and Quarter Avenue." They were practically there, if they just turned the corner. He wouldn't even have to fly. But there was Sebastian, looking up at him, waiting for him to leave again, and trying not to cry. He felt between them the sway of a fragile skein of love, like a spider's web that links the branches of two trees in a forest. On the other hand, there was the nylon line that reeled him back, again and again, to the city of people that he loved.

He got down so he was eye to eye with his son. He pulled him in and kissed the place where the curls fell over his eyebrows, and Sebastian squirmed, but for once didn't protest. Jack thought about what he could live with and what he couldn't live without.

"I'm so sorry, Chief," said Jack. He placed his phone in his pocket.

Sebastian put his sticky palms up to Jack's cheeks. "Are you crying, Daddy?" he asked.

"Do you know how much I love you?" he told the boy.

Sebastian bit his lip.

"I love you more than the world." He reached down and picked Sebastian up in his arms. He hardly weighed anything. And then he bent his knees and looked up, and when he jumped, the sky caught him, and they were soaring. Above the buildings, and up, up, up, away.

"See Yume Kitasei's story "Super" online at
Metaphorosis.
*If you liked it, leave a comment. Authors love
that!
Remember to subscribe to our e-mail updates so
you'll know when new stories are posted."*

About the story

Confession: once, when I was a teenager babysitting a toddler, I decided to try to tire him out by making him climb twelve flights of stairs. We'd been playing all morning, and I was hoping by the time we got to the top, he'd be all ready to nap until his parents came home. Mind you, this was a big baby. Big enough that he could climb stairs at all while his age-peers were still crawling. He took each step with great seriousness and intent, and when we got to the twelfth floor, I was panting and ready to lie down — and he was ready to keep going.

Children have incredible energy. I don't know how anyone keeps up with them. Now that I'm at the age where a lot of my friends are having them, I enjoy being the auntie who swoops in to babysit for a few hours, change a few diapers, wipe away tears, play pretend. And I have just enough experience to think that every parent must have superpowers of their own.

This story popped into my mind fully-formed one day when I was with one of my friends and his son. My friend is a wonderful father with enormous patience (note to friend: the main character is not based on you). But as the day progressed, he got more and more tired, because that is how adult humans work; his son, on the other hand, got more and more wound up. By the end, my friend was operating at 5mph and his son was operating at 60mph.

This is what I was trying to capture with this story: that feeling of caring for young children you love, while feeling worn out, ragged, and less and less able to keep up with them. I also wanted to look at how a person's priorities can change when you have a child — in this case, under extraordinary circumstances. If you are a superhero, can you really put your city before your child? What if you really have to choose? And what does that feel like? Well, you'll have to read my story to see what I think the answer to that is!

A question for the author

Q: Where do you write?

A: Where I write is really a factor of when I write. My job can keep me busy, so I have to seize the fifteen to thirty-minute chunks whenever I can. In fact, I get some of my best writing done on the subway standing up, wedged between one person's pointy elbow and another 's backpack (oof, dude), tap-tapping away with two thumbs. I'll start in the early morning on my laptop on a small green table in my bedroom while eating breakfast, email my work in progress to myself so I can continue on my phone on the way to work, and then end my day sprawled on the living room couch to finish it out for the night.

So short answer: everywhere, anywhen.

About the author

Yume Kitasei lives in Brooklyn, NY with two terrible cats, Filibuster and Boondoggle. She believes everyone has a super power. Hers is the ability to make the perfect cup of coffee.

www.yumekitasei.com, @YumeKitasei

Copyright

Metaphorosis Publishing

Metaphorosis offers beautifully written science fiction and fantasy. Our imprints include:

Metaphorosis Magazine
plant based press
Metaphorosis Books
Driftwyrd
Vestige

Help keep Metaphorosis running at
Patreon.com/metaphorosis

See more about some of our books on the following pages.

Metaphorosis Magazine

Metaphorosis

a magazine of speculative fiction

Metaphorosis is an online speculative fiction magazine dedicated to quality writing. We publish an original story every week, along with author bios, interviews, and notes on story origins. Come and see us online at magazine.Metaphorosis.com

Keep Metaphorosis running! Support us at
Patreon.com/metaphorosis

You can also find us at:
Twitter: @MetaphorosisMag,
@MetaphorosisRev, @Metaphorosis
Facebook:
www.facebook.com/metaphorosis

We publish monthly print and e-book issues, as well as yearly Best of and Complete anthologies.

Metaphorosis:
Best of 2018

The best science fiction and fantasy stories from *Metaphorosis* magazine's third year.

Metaphorosis
2018

All the stories from *Metaphorosis* magazine's third year. Fifty-two great SFF stories.

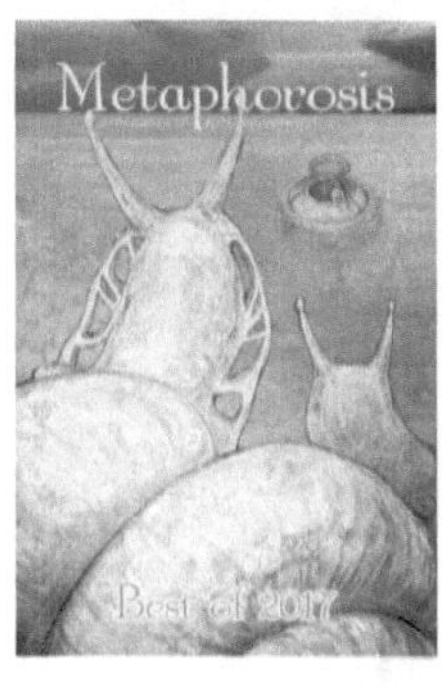

Metaphorosis: Best of 2017

The best science fiction and fantasy stories from *Metaphorosis* magazine's *second* year.

Metaphorosis 2017

All the stories from *Metaphorosis* magazine's second year. Fifty-three great SFF stories.

Metaphorosis: Best of 2016

The best science fiction and fantasy stories from *Metaphorosis* magazine's first year.

Metaphorosis 2016

Almost all the stories from *Metaphorosis* magazine's first year.

Plant Based Press

Vegan-friendly science fiction and fantasy, including an annual anthology of the year's best SFF stories.

Best Vegan SFF of 2018

The best vegan science fiction and fantasy stories of 2018!

Best Vegan SFF of 2017

The best vegan science fiction and fantasy stories of 2017!

Best Vegan SFF of 2016

The best vegan science fiction and fantasy stories of 2016!

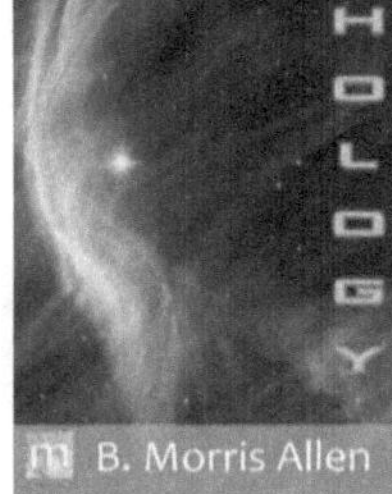

Susurrus

A darkly romantic story of magic, love, and suffering.

Allenthology: Volume I

A quarter century of SFF, including the full contents of three separate collections.

Metaphorosis Books

Science fiction and fantasy books for writers – full of great stories, but with an additional focus on the craft of speculative fiction writing.

Score

an SFF symphony

What if stories were written like music? *Score* is an anthology of varied stories arranged to follow an emotional score from the heights of joy to the depths of despair – but always with a little hope shining through.

Reading 5X5

Five stories, five times

Twenty-five SFF authors, five base stories, five versions of each – see how different writers take on the same material, with stories in contemporary and high fantasy, soft and hard SF, and a mysterious 'other' category.

Reading 5X5

Writers' Edition

All the stories from the regular, readers' edition, plus two extra stories, the story seed, and authors' notes on writing. Over 100 pages of additional material specifically aimed at writers.

9 781640 761506